Casually Tab leaned against the fence beside Aiden. "It almost sounds like you're asking me to help."

"Does it, now?"

"You bet it does. It's almost like we're investigating. Both of us. Together." She covered her smug grin by draining the last of her coffee. "I seem to recall something you said about not wanting my help because it was too... What was it you said? It was too dangerous for a delicate flower like me."

"I'm real sure I never called you a flower."

"I added that part," she said. "You know what you said."

He shoved away from the fence and stood tall before her. "If you're done with your I-told-you-so, I'd like to put things into motion."

"And you want me to help you investigate." She looked up through her eyelashes.

"I reckon I do."

USA TODAY Bestselling Author

CASSIE MILES

MONTANA MIDWIFE

HARLEQUIN®
entertain, enrich, inspire™

In memory of Rosemary Heiser. She will be missed.

Recycling programs
for this product may
not exist in your area.

ISBN-13: 978-0-373-74705-4

MONTANA MIDWIFE

Copyright © 2012 by Kay Bergstrom

www.Harlequin.com

Printed in U.S.A.

ABOUT THE AUTHOR

Though born in Chicago and raised in L.A., *USA TODAY* bestselling author Cassie Miles has lived in Colorado long enough to be considered a semi-native. The first home she owned was a log cabin in the mountains overlooking Elk Creek, with a thirty-mile commute to her work at the *Denver Post*.

After raising two daughters and cooking tons of macaroni and cheese for her family, Cassie is trying to be more adventurous in her culinary efforts. Ceviche, anyone? She's discovered that almost anything tastes better with wine. When she's not plotting Harlequin Intrigue books, Cassie likes to hang out at the Denver Botanical Gardens near her high-rise home.

Books by Cassie Miles

CAST OF CHARACTERS

Tab (Tabitha) Willows—The half-Crow midwife can't escape her past when she returns to the Little Big Horn country where she grew up.

Aiden Gabriel—The family ranch is his home, but the helicopter rescue service is his dream job.

Misty Gabriel—Aiden's pregnant, seventeen-year-old sister needs Tab's help to deliver her baby and to rescue her from a murder charge.

Clinton Brown—The father of Misty's baby is more intelligent than he looks. What else is he hiding?

Sylvia Gabriel—Aiden and Misty's mother.

Blake Henry—The ranch foreman and Sylvia's longtime lover.

Maria Spotted Bear—Tab's grandma lives on the reservation and knows a lot about tribal medicine.

Joseph Lefthand—The chief of the Crow Reservation police.

Sheriff Steve Fielding—The sheriff works with the tribal police to catch a possible serial killer.

David Welling—He loved Misty until the day he was murdered.

Bert Welling—David's fastidious uncle owns the gas station in town and employs many of the local kids.

Ellen Jessop—Misty's friend/enemy appears to be a victim of the serial killer.

Aspen Jim Sherman—The troubles started when this flashy con man moved to town.

Wally the Buffalo Man—The old homeless man has made a life for himself by camping on the reservation.

Chuck Longbeak and Woody Silas—Like the rest of the people in town, these young men believe Misty is guilty of murder.

Chapter One

On a high ridge overlooking the Little Big Horn River, Tab Willows sat up straight in the saddle and lifted her arm above her head. Finally, she had a signal for her cell phone. There was no way she could find Misty and her boyfriend unless they gave her better directions to their location. This horse didn't come equipped with GPS.

She hit the redial.

Misty Gabriel answered immediately. "Tab, where are you? I need you."

Panic trembled in her voice, which was understandable for a woman in labor with her first baby. For some unexplainable reason, Misty and Clinton had decided to go off-roading and had gotten their vehicle stuck in a creek bed that was damp with melt from a recent snow. The early November weather wasn't bad right now, but night was coming. With the darkness came an icy chill.

Tab hadn't been working with Misty as a regular client in her midwife practice, but she felt an obligation and a connection to this young woman she used to babysit, even though, as adults, they didn't appear to have much in common. Misty was the spoiled seventeen-year-old daughter of a wealthy ranching family. Bubbly and blonde, she giggled with every other breath. In contrast, Tab seldom laughed out loud. Her overall appearance—dusky-colored skin and straight black hair worn in a single braid down to her waist—favored her mother's Crow heritage. Her blue eyes came from her dad.

"I'm looking down at the area you described," Tab said, "but I don't see your Jeep. Give me directions."

"Like what?" She giggled nervously. "It's not like there are street signs or anything."

Focus, Misty. "Any unusual rock formations?"

"Oh, yeah. On the other side of the river and up a slope, there's a big cave we used to play in when we were kids."

"Half-Moon Cave."

That landmark told Tab the approximate whereabouts. When Misty had first called, she'd said there were no passable roads, which was why Tab was on horseback. She wished she'd taken her van; there was a decent route that ran fairly close to Misty's location.

"Half-Moon Cave, that's right." Her giggle broke into a sob. "You've got to hurry. Clinton hit his head."

Of course, he did. This situation just got worse and worse. "Is he conscious?"

"Kind of. He was trying to push the Jeep out of the mud and he slipped and conked his forehead on the bumper."

On horseback, there was no way to evacuate a man with a concussion and a woman in labor. "Let's talk about you. How far apart are your pains?"

"I don't know. It just hurts."

"And how many months along are you?"

"Eight-ish. The doctor said I could have the baby any time now."

In the best-case scenario, Misty was experiencing Braxton Hicks contractions that wouldn't lead to childbirth. Or she could be going into early labor. "I want you to stay calm. Take slow, steady breaths, okay?"

"Whatever you say, Tab."

"One thing I don't understand," she said. "Why didn't you call your brother to come for you?"

Her brother, Aiden Gabriel, provided a private rescue-helicopter service for the local hospitals, the sheriff and national park rescue teams. Because he also worked on the family ranch, he wasn't always available, but Tab knew that Aiden would drop everything to rescue his baby sister.

"Aiden is a big old jerk," Misty said. "And he doesn't like Clinton."

An opinion Tab could easily comprehend. Clinton had taken his very pregnant girlfriend on an off-road adventure, gotten them stuck and then knocked himself unconscious. Clearly, he wasn't the sharpest arrow in the quiver. "Brace yourself, Misty. I'm calling your brother. You need his help."

"Maybe not. I think I see somebody coming."

"Stay where you are," Tab said sharply. "I can't find you if you go wandering off."

"Okay. See you later, elevator."

"Real soon, harvest moon."

Tab smiled as she remembered the rhyming games she and Misty played ten years ago. Tab had been sixteen. Her life had been split between living with her dad in Billings and with her grandma, Maria Spotted Bear, on the Crow reservation. When her dad had been hired to do contracting work at the Gabriel ranch near Henley, she'd tagged along and had gotten recruited as a live-in babysitter for seven-year-old Misty.

That summer had been a rough time for the Gabriel family. Misty's dad had been killed in a car accident. Tab felt like she could understand Misty's grief because she'd lost her mom and knew what it was like to have a parent die too young. She and Misty had bonded but their friendship wasn't the main thing that happened that summer. That summer, Tab had fallen in love for the first time.

Looking down at her cell phone, she remembered the tall, lean, handsome Aiden Gabriel with his thick brown hair and his dreamy gray eyes. He'd been twenty-one when he came home from college and shouldered the responsibilities of a ranch owner, helping his mom to cope when her husband died. Though Tab never told anyone, she'd dreamed of Aiden every night, imagining his kiss and what it would feel like to be held in his strong arms. Once, he'd given her a necklace with a shiny four-leaf clover pendant, which she'd worn for years before tucking it away in her jewelry box.

Tab hadn't spoken to Aiden since moving back to this area, but she'd seen him recently at a meeting in Crow Agency where the topic was the ongoing law enforcement problems on the reservation. After noticing that he was still the best-looking cowboy she'd ever seen, she'd grabbed one of his business cards and recorded his number on her phone to use in case of birthing emergencies. This circumstance qualified. She hit the speed dial.

On the third ring, he answered, "This is Aiden Gabriel."

"Hi, it's Tab." A pause stretched between them. He didn't remember her. And wasn't that a knife to the gut? She clarified, "Tab Willows. I saw you at that law enforcement meeting in Crow Agency and took your card."

"Tabitha." He was one of the few people who used her full name. "You haven't been around for a while. I heard you were at nursing school in Missoula."

"That's right." Hearing his voice cast her backward in time to when she was a lovesick teenager wishing on a star that he'd notice her. She swallowed hard. "I'm a midwife."

"We have some catching up to do."

Tongue-tied, she mumbled, "Guess so."

"It's been a long time, but I'll never forget that pretty, young girl with long black hair who used to race my fastest horse across the fields bareback."

He'd thought she was pretty? If he'd told her when she was sixteen, she would have exploded in a wild burst of angst and joy. Even now, his compliment made it hard for her to breathe. "Misty needs your help."

"What happened?"

"She called me because she's having labor pains. She and her boyfriend got their Jeep stuck in a creek bed, and she needs to be evacuated."

"Are you with her?"

"On my way," Tab said. "But I can't bring her in because I'm on horseback. Misty said they were near Half-Moon Cave."

"I know where it is," he said. "Tabitha, I hope you remember what was discussed at that meeting. If you're riding alone, you should be prepared for trouble."

In her work, she often traveled alone, heading

to remote locations to work with women in labor. And she didn't take unnecessary chances. A rifle scabbard was tucked under her saddlebags. "I'm armed."

"See you there."

With her cell phone tucked into the pocket of her brown denim jacket, she flicked the reins and nudged her heel into the flank of Shua, her grandma's blue-black mare with the white blaze on her forehead. With minimal direction, the horse descended from the ridge and galloped across a wide valley dotted with patches of old snow.

As she directed Shua uphill through a stand of pine trees, she wondered how she could arrange to ride back to the hospital in the helicopter with Aiden. Unfortunately, she couldn't abandon her horse, even though Shua could probably find her own way back to the corral outside her grandma's house. The chopper ride would have to wait for another day.

If she took Misty as a client, she'd have plenty of opportunity to see Aiden. Not that she needed an excuse. Her midwife work made it important to know the emergency providers. She had every reason to call him and set a coffee date or invite him to her grandma's house and bake him a pie. Did he still like apple? Would he still think she was pretty?

A blast of gunfire echoed through the canyons and across the fields. Three shots.

Shua reared back. Tab's memories and daydreams shattered. There was trouble ahead.

If her reckoning was correct, Half-Moon Cave was just over the next rise. She urged her horse to go faster. From the hilltop, she looked down at a field near the canyon walls and saw the open-top Jeep with the rear tires buried up to the hubcaps in the mud. Taking her rifle from the scabbard, Tab held it to her shoulder and peered through the scope for a better look at the vehicle. There was a man sprawled in the backseat; she couldn't tell if he'd been shot. Misty was nowhere in sight.

This couldn't be good. Tab cocked her rifle and fired into the air. Her gunfire would warn off attackers and let Misty know that help was on the way.

Two more shots answered hers.

Rifle in hand, Tab rode fast. Her long braid bounced against her back, and the wind streamed across her cheeks. Her protective instincts came to the fore as she remembered the vulnerable child she babysat so long ago.

Approaching the Jeep, she shouted, "Misty?"

Loud sobbing came from a tangle of willows and cottonwoods that bordered the river. Still on horseback, Tab approached. If any real marksmanship was required, she'd need to dismount and brace herself. Right now, she wanted the option of fast maneuvering on Shua.

"Misty, are you all right?"

"I'm over here."

In a small clearing, Tab saw the body of a man who had been shot in the chest. His jacket hung open. His eyes stared blankly at the darkening sky. He wasn't moving.

Kneeling on the ground beside him was Misty. She held her bloody hands in front of her as though afraid to touch anything. A rifle lay on the ground.

Misty turned her tear-streaked face toward her. "I didn't kill him. I swear I didn't."

THOUGH AIDEN WAS ALWAYS on call for emergencies, it usually took a while for him to get started because he had to drive to the air field in Henley to pick up his six-passenger helicopter, a Bell Long Ranger. Today, he needed only to walk from the barn to the helipad near his cabin at the Gabriel family ranch. Earlier today, he'd given piloting lessons to a couple of the ranch hands. With winter coming, there wasn't as much work for the cowboys to do, and Aiden could use some part-time help with his newly established rescue business.

Less than fifteen minutes after Tabitha's call, he was in the cockpit. He fastened his seat belt, depressed the starter, checked the fuel-pressure gauge, opened the throttle and pointed the nose toward the southeast. If he'd been following roads, the drive to Half-Moon Cave near the Little Big Horn

River would have taken nearly an hour. Swooping through the sky cut his arrival time to approximately twenty minutes. Top speed was necessary. From what Tabitha had told him, Misty might be giving birth at any moment.

He hadn't been pleased when his baby sister turned up pregnant. Misty was fourteen years younger than he was, not much more than a child herself. Aiden still had a hard time thinking of her as a mother, but the idea of having a nephew had grown on him.

As his mom constantly pointed out, it was time for a new generation in the Gabriel family. Mom would have preferred a marriage before the baby, but she'd take what she could get, especially since it didn't look like Aiden would be heading toward the altar any time soon. His long-distance relationship had fizzled last month when they'd argued about where to spend Christmas. Aiden had point-blank refused to make the trip to Los Angeles to hang tinsel on palm trees, and his lady had no interest in coming to the ranch. The breakup had been inevitable. They'd grown apart.

Using his headset, he put through a call to Tabitha's cell phone. When she answered, he clarified his directions. "I think I'm getting close. I'm following the course of the river."

"We're on the east side. Near a dried-up creek. Please hurry, Aiden."

He heard the note of urgency in her voice. "What's wrong? Is it the baby?"

"Misty is fine." She paused. "There's been a shooting."

"Are you safe?"

"I think the shooter took off, but I can't be sure."

"I'll be there in a few minutes," he said. "Tell me when you hear me getting close."

"I think we're okay," she said. "We took cover by the river."

He leaned forward as though his will could force the chopper to fly faster. The landscape below was a rugged sea of dry field grass and clumps of sage brush. "Did you see the gunman?"

"I can barely hear you, Aiden."

"Stay on the line." Like a 911 operator, he needed to maintain contact so he'd be aware of the situation. "What can you tell me?"

"Not much. Misty will have to do the explaining."

A shooter had come after his sister? His grip tensed on the cyclic stick as he swerved to the left. He never expected anything like this, never thought violence would reach out and touch his family. "Was anyone shot?"

"Yes," she said tersely. "It's not Misty or her boyfriend. Somebody else."

"Is he seriously wounded?"

"I really can't hear you," Tabitha said.

"Don't hang up. Keep the line open."

He should have expected something like this. Law enforcement had become a serious problem in the area, especially on the Crow reservation. Tribal lands spread across nearly two and a half million acres with only a handful of officers and a couple of agents from the Bureau of Indian Affairs to keep order. And the situation in Henley wasn't much better. Budget cuts had sliced the police and sheriff's department to the bare bone.

At the meeting in Crow Agency, the tribal police told them to be on the lookout for two girls from Henley who were last seen on the rez before they went missing. Nobody mentioned the possibility of a serial killer, but the threat was implied. Both of the missing girls were blondes like Misty.

"Aiden, I can hear your chopper."

On the opposite side of the river, he saw the sandstone cliffs and rock formations. "I'm near Half-Moon Cave."

"Do you see us? Do you see the Jeep?"

He spotted Clinton's open-top vehicle stuck in the creek bed. Beside it was a black horse. Relief flooded through him when he saw Misty in her bright pink jacket step out from the cover of the trees and wave with both arms. She was safe. For now.

Chapter Two

Aiden stood over the body of a man who wasn't much older than his sister. The fresh blood on his shirt made a vivid splash of crimson against the dry prairie grass in the clearing. The wind sighed through the bare branches of trees, and the rushing of the river played a quiet dirge. The family and friends of this young man would mourn his passing. Out of respect for them and for the victim, Aiden spread a tarp from the helicopter over the body.

He stood and took a step back.

His sister had a talent for getting into trouble, but this went beyond her usual. When he turned, he saw Misty was standing by the Jeep with her boyfriend. This time, she'd gotten herself involved in a murder. There would be consequences.

Before landing, he'd done an aerial sweep of the area and had seen nothing that appeared threatening. In the afternoon sunlight, his vision extended for miles in every direction. He hadn't spotted the shooter fleeing or hiding among the rocks and brush. There were no signs of a getaway vehicle, which didn't surprise Aiden. Almost an hour had passed since the first phone call from Tabitha; that was plenty of time for a shooter to put distance between himself and the scene of the crime.

If there was a shooter...

As he moved to the edge of the clearing, Tabitha joined him. "I'm glad you covered him," she said. "I wasn't sure if that would disturb evidence."

"We aren't exactly dealing with a crack team of CSI investigators." He'd done enough work with local law enforcement to know the drill. "The police will be more concerned with obvious stuff. That's Misty's rifle on the ground. Do you know how it got here?"

"You need to ask her."

"There's a smear of blood on the stock."

"When I arrived," Tabitha said, "Misty was kneeling beside the body. I think she was trying to help. She had blood on her hands."

"Do you think she did it?" He asked the question of the sky and the hills and the river. "Do you think she killed that young man?"

"I don't know."

Though he wasn't sure what he'd do, Aiden had to know the truth. "Misty isn't a murderer."

"No, she's not."

For the first time since he'd landed, he looked directly at Tabitha. Her blue-eyed gaze was disconcerting, partly because the color was unexpected and partly because she was a lot prettier than he remembered with high cheekbones and a strong, stubborn chin. Her long black braid glistened in the fading sunlight. Though he should have been focused on his sister and the murdered man, this beautiful woman distracted him. His fingers itched to unfasten her braid and caress her silky hair.

"There is a plus side," she said. "Emergency medical evacuation isn't necessary. Not for Misty, anyway."

He watched her full lips as she spoke. "Does that mean she isn't in labor?"

"I haven't done a full exam, obviously. But her mysterious labor pains seem to have disappeared, and she's a month away from her due date. I advised her to check with her doctor in case there are complications. She might need to be on bed rest."

"I like that idea." With an effort, he reined in his inappropriate thoughts about Tabitha's long legs and slender waist. "It'd be nice to keep Misty close to home before the baby comes."

"I'm more concerned about Clinton." Her crisp, professional tone helped create a distance between them. "I patched up his head wound, but he's had a concussion and needs to be under observation."

"I understand." But he didn't agree. He could have cited five or six times when he'd been knocked unconscious and had survived just fine. "I'm mighty glad you got here when you did. This situation could have been worse. Not that there's anything worse than murder."

Even if his sister was the killer? Surely, there was an explanation. Self-defense?

"We should call the sheriff," Tabitha said.

"But this is reservation land. That means we call the Crow police chief, Joseph Lefthand. I've worked with him before. He's good at his job."

"I agree. Joseph is a good, dedicated lawman."

He took out his cell phone. "I'll call him."

"Wait," she said. "The tribal police don't have the resources to process forensic evidence, and I want to make sure the investigation is done right. This isn't a straightforward murder."

"It's not that complicated." He didn't need to go into detail about how his aerial sweep failed to show evidence of a killer on the run, or how Misty's rifle was on the ground beside the body. "We're looking at an obvious case of self-defense."

"That's not what Misty says."

"Do you believe her, Tabitha?"

"I do. Your sister might be irresponsible, but she's not a liar." She arched an eyebrow. "Please call me Tab. The only other person who uses my full name is my grandma, and that's only when she's mad at me."

Her slight smile made him want to see a full-fledged grin and to hear her laughter. "I remember your grandma. Maria Spotted Bear." He looked past the Jeep to where a black mare was grazing. "Is that her horse?"

"Shua," Tab said. "Don't ask me why a black horse is named with the Crow word for blue. Grandma has her reasons."

"Is she well?"

"According to her, she's in great health. But she's been diagnosed with a touch of congenital heart failure. A couple of months ago, she fainted and broke her wrist. One of the reasons I moved back here was to take care of her."

"Sorry to hear that she's ailing."

Tab shrugged. A simple gesture, but he found it charming. "How's Sylvia?"

"Mom is strong as an ox. It's hard to believe she's almost sixty."

A silence stretched between them. Much had happened in the ten years they'd been out of contact. Though he'd never been a real chatty sort of guy, he had an urge to tell her everything about his life, his hopes and his dreams. With so much to say, he didn't know where to start.

Tab took the first step. "Let's talk to your sister, and then we can decide who to call."

Together, they returned to the Jeep where Misty leaned against the front bumper with her arms cradling her belly. Clinton stood beside her. He'd slapped his cowboy hat onto his head, almost covering the gauze bandage that Tab had applied.

"I know what you're thinking," Clinton said. "I should have protected my girl. But I was out cold."

"And you didn't see anything," Aiden said.

"No, sir."

He turned to his sister. "I'm guessing that you were attacked. Maybe this guy—"

"David Welling." There was a hitch in her voice. "His name is David Welling."

"Okay, David Welling came at you, maybe he—"

"I can't believe he's dead."

"Calm down, sweetie. Take a nice, slow, deep breath." He waited until she'd composed herself before he continued, "It's not your fault. You had to shoot David in self-defense."

"I didn't shoot anybody." She shook her head, and her curly blond hair whipped across her face. "I never would shoot anybody."

Aiden exchanged a glance with Tab. She'd warned him that his sister's story was complicated. "Take your time, Misty. Tell me exactly what happened."

"I was waiting for Tab. I heard a noise over by the river, and I got my rifle out of the back of the Jeep. I was scared that somebody might come after us. Poor Clinton was unconscious, and I couldn't let anybody hurt him."

"Whoa," Clinton said. "I'm not helpless. I could've got to my feet and taken care of you."

Aiden held up his hand, signaling Clinton to stop. "I'm listening to Misty, now."

She continued, "As soon as I got a little bit closer—"

"Did you take the rifle with you?"

"I left it right here." She pointed to the front bumper. "I figured that if I needed it, I could run back and grab it real quick."

"But I thought you were trying to protect Clinton?"

She tapped her foot. "Do you want to hear this, or not, Aiden?"

Understanding her motivations was like asking a chicken why it pecked in the dirt. "Go on."

"I recognized David. I dated him before he graduated high school and moved away from Henley."

As far as Aiden could tell, she'd dated most of the male population of Henley High, which made it even more astounding that she'd ended up with a pea brain like Clinton. "Is this David Welling any relation to Bert Welling who runs a gas station in Henley?"

"Bert is his uncle," Misty said. "David used to pump gas for Bert before he moved to Billings with his dad. Anyway, when I saw him standing there in the clearing, I said hi. And he said I shouldn't be here, and I told him that we were stuck, and he said I needed to get away from here, to get the hell away from here."

Her eyes welled up with tears. "Then I heard the shots. David grabbed his chest and fell down. And there was blood. Oh my God, there was a lot of blood."

"Did you see who shot him?"

"I hit the dirt. I thought they were shooting at me. I covered my head and I thought about my baby. I couldn't let anything bad happen to my baby, I just couldn't."

Her hands flew up to cover her face as heavy sobs shook her shoulders. For once, Clinton did the right thing, stepping forward to comfort her and hold her against his chest. His protective attitude made Aiden wonder if there was something Misty had left out of her story.

Clinton might have been the shooter. Misty could be claiming responsibility to keep her boyfriend from being a suspect. But that didn't make sense. A self-defense plea worked just as well for Clinton as for Misty. Aiden doubted that either one of them would be charged with murder…except for one hitch. The victim appeared to be unarmed.

As Misty's sobs abated, Aiden asked, "Why was your rifle in the clearing?"

"I ran back to get it, but the gun wasn't where I left it."

"Where was it?"

"Right about here." She pointed to a clump of sagebrush that was about twenty yards from the clearing. "I could tell it had been fired."

"Are you saying that the killer used your rifle?"

"I don't know."

"Did you see him?" he asked.

"He must have run off."

Or maybe he turned invisible. Aiden was getting more and more frustrated with her story. "How long between when you heard the shot and ran back to get the rifle?"

"I don't know."

"Think, Misty."

Tears streaked down her cheeks. "Don't be so mean to me."

"I can help," Tab said. "When I heard the first shot, I was on the other side of those hills. It took five or six minutes before I got to the crest and could see the Jeep. Clinton was unconscious in the backseat. I fired a warning shot in the air to scare off anybody who might be hanging around."

"I shot back," Misty said. "I didn't aim at anything. I was just shooting in the air. Twice."

Aiden fitted the pieces together. According to his sister, a mysterious shooter had killed David Welling using her rifle, and then disappeared within five minutes. He gauged the distance from where she found the rifle to the trees and shrubs that bordered the river. Though it was possible that the killer could make that dash, it was unlikely. Why use Misty's rifle? Why choose this particular moment to kill David Welling? And what was Welling doing out here in the first place?

After patting his sister on the arm and offering reassurances that he hoped weren't empty, Aiden pulled Tab to one side. His senses registered the clean fragrance of her shampoo and the warmth that emanated from her body, but he kept his mind trained on the problem at hand.

"You're right," he said to Tab. "This investigation is beyond the resources of the tribal police. But we still need to contact Joseph Lefthand."

"I'm not sure of the procedure," she said.

He explained. First, they needed to notify tribal police of a crime committed on their land. In most cases, the Crow were happy to pass on the problem and cede jurisdiction through an agent of the federal government, namely someone from the Bureau of Indian Affairs. Then the county sheriff would take over.

"I hope the sheriff can get started with his investigation before dark." She looked toward the sun sinking in the west. "There might be footprints from the gunman. Or evidence of his vehicle."

"If Misty's story is accurate," he said, "ballistics will show that the bullets came from her rifle."

"There might be fingerprints."

"In addition to Misty's prints." She'd already said

that she fired the gun and would, therefore, have gunshot residue on her clothes.

He wished that his sister had come up with a more convincing story—something about how David Welling attacked her, and she was forced to defend herself. The idea of a murderer who could appear out of nowhere and vanish in the blink of an eye was improbable. It sounded like a lie. And lying made Misty look as if she had something to hide.

If this investigation went wrong, it was entirely possible that his sister would be delivering her baby in jail.

Chapter Three

While Aiden and Clinton messed around with the Jeep, trying to dig out the rear tires, Tab took a striped wool blanket from her saddlebags and handed it to Misty. "Spread this on the ground. Choose a spot that's out of the wind."

"Why?"

"You might as well get comfortable. It's going to take a while for the authorities to get here."

Definitely an understatement. When Aiden had put through calls to the tribal police, the BIA and the sheriff, she'd heard the growing frustration in his voice. Everybody promised to respond just as soon as they could, which meant they had other business to clean off their plates.

Though Tab thought that murder should take precedence, she was accustomed to bureaucracy. There was nothing to do but wait. She dug through her saddlebag, ignoring the medical equipment, and found a square plastic container packed with more practical supplies.

"All this waiting around sucks," Misty said. She turned her gaze toward the clearing where the body lay covered by a tarp. "But I won't leave. I owe it to David to talk to the sheriff. I'm the only witness."

And the most obvious suspect. In spite of the giggles and the frequent flipping of her blond hair, Misty wasn't a fool. The girl had to realize how implausible her story about the vanishing gunman sounded. She had to know that she could be charged with murder.

Tab followed her to a spot beside a low flat rock and helped her lay the blanket over the dried prairie grass. "Tell me about David."

"We only went out on one date. There wasn't any kissing or anything." Misty gave her a conspiratorial grin. "Can I tell you a secret? You have to promise not to let Aiden know."

As Tab felt herself being drawn more deeply into the situation, her defenses rose. The smart move would be to back off. She was a midwife, not a policewoman. A murder investigation wasn't her problem. But her heart wouldn't let her abandon Misty. "Does your secret have anything to do with David Welling's death?"

"No way," Misty said.

"Then I won't tell anybody else. I promise. Wild horses won't drag it out of me."

"In sophomore year at Henley High, me and Lisa and Heather made a bet. Whoever was the first to date every guy in the junior and senior class was the winner."

"Why juniors and seniors? You were sopho-mores."

"The boys our age were dorks, and most of them didn't have their driver's licenses. That's why we went for the older guys. Our bet wasn't as wild as it sounds. There were only seventy-six guys total in both classes."

Their bet sounded like a sure way to get into trouble. Tab imagined these three little heartbreak-ers sowing havoc at Henley High. "What counted as a date?"

"The guy had to invite you. It could be a study date or a ski trip or going to a party. Or they had to buy you something, like if you went out in a group and they paid for your burger."

"What happened with you and David?"

"He was fixing a flat tire for me at his uncle's gas station—"

"Wait a minute. How old were you?"

"Not old enough to have my license, if that's what you're getting at."

"You stole the car?"

"Borrowed it from Aiden. He was too busy run-ning the ranch and learning how to pilot his chop-per to be worried about me." She rolled her eyes. "Geez, Tab. I started driving around on the ranch as soon as I was big enough to see over the steering wheel. You know how it is."

"I do." Tab had attended high school in Billings—a city where regulations were enforced. Though Henley was less than fifty miles away, she knew that different rules applied. "So, you and David were at the gas station. Then what?"

"We got to talking. I barely knew him. He was really shy and quiet, didn't play football or basketball. But he had a real cute smile."

"And you started flirting."

"He bought me an orange soda." She giggled. "He asked me out, too. But I turned him down."

"Why?"

"When he bought the soda, I could cross him off my list. And he was nice, you know. I didn't want to lead him on."

Tab was glad to hear that Misty had a conscience, after all. "Who won the bet?"

"Nobody. We all found boyfriends, and we didn't want to be with anybody else. It's funny, you know. I probably never would have gone out with Clinton if it hadn't been for that bet. And now, he's my baby's daddy."

"And you're happy about that?"

"You bet I am." Misty positioned herself on the blanket with her legs tucked under. With her pregnant belly, she looked like a blond Buddha. "This is a nice, thick blanket. Why did you bring it along?"

"When you first called and said you were in labor, I thought I might be delivering your baby out here."

"Oh. My. God. That is so totally not sanitary."

Tab didn't bother with a long, thoughtful explanation about how childbirth was a natural process not an illness that required hospitalization. Midwifery was her lifework, and she didn't feel a need to justify her profession. Some people got it. Others didn't.

"My ancestors have been having babies without hospitals for a very long time. So have yours."

"I guess you're right. The Gabriels have been ranching in this area since the early 1900s. I don't guess there were many hospitals back then."

An accurate assumption, but Tab was fairly certain that Misty's great-grandmother had the best care that money could buy. The Gabriels had a history of wealth and power that held true to the present day. Their cattle ranch provided employment for many people in the area. The family reputation might work in Misty's favor when it came to murder charges, but Tab suspected that there were those who resented the Gabriel clan and would take perverse pleasure in seeing Misty behind bars.

"I want to talk to you about stress," Tab said.

"Okay."

"When you're pregnant," Tab said, "it's not good

for you to be under a lot of stress. That means it's not good for your baby, either."

"What can I do? Is there some kind of herb I can take?"

Many natural remedies were used to encourage labor, but Misty wasn't at that point. "You're already taking prenatal vitamins, right? And probably extra iron."

Misty bobbed her head. "And I'm drinking herbal teas, mostly chamomile. I like doing organic stuff. I made Clinton take a class on natural childbirth that they were teaching at the hospital in Henley."

"Good for you." Tab squatted at the edge of the blanket and opened the plastic container she'd brought from her saddlebags. "Those breathing techniques are also useful for dealing with stress. Concentrate on inhaling and exhaling. Do you ever meditate?"

"You mean like yoga? Nope, that's not my thing."

"What helps you slow down and relax?" Tab assumed from Misty's confused expression that slowing down wasn't part of her agenda. "How about music? Do you listen to music?"

"All the time." She dug into her jacket pocket and pulled out a tiny player attached to ear buds. "Mostly country and western. Is that unstressful?"

"Better than heavy metal," Tab said. "When you feel yourself getting tight inside, just plug in your music, close your eyes and tune out all the other distractions."

From the plastic container, she unpacked a simple picnic of crackers, cheese, jerky, an apple and a six-pack of bottled water. Misty pounced on the jerky. "You're a mind reader, Tab. I was starving."

Working with pregnant women taught her that she couldn't go wrong with healthy snacks. "Dig in before the guys figure out that there's food over here."

Aiden's effort to get the Jeep unstuck had deteriorated to walking about the vehicle, scratching his head and scowling. Clinton was doing much the same. Very likely, they'd come to the conclusion that when the sheriff got here, they could hook up a winch.

Sitting back on her heels, Tab watched as Misty devoured a chunk of jerky, took a huge swig from the water bottle and gave a loud burp followed by a giggle. "Sorry," Misty said. "That was gross."

"A little bit."

"My body keeps doing this weird stuff. I have to pee all the time."

"Can you feel the baby kicking?"

"I can." A happy smile brightened her face. "That part is really cool."

Tab was reminded of the seven-year-old she used to babysit. That summer had been rough on the girl. Not only had she lost her father, but her mother had been so devastated that she could barely drag herself out of bed. And Aiden had been preoccupied with the day-to-day operations at the ranch. Throughout, Misty maintained a relentlessly cheerful attitude to hide her pain and vulnerability.

"I wish I could stay here and wait with you," Tab said, "but I need to leave soon."

Misty nodded as she screwed the top back onto the water bottle. When she looked up, her eyes were troubled. "Can I ask you something?"

"Anything."

"Am I going to jail?"

Tab couldn't promise a good outcome. Even if Misty was completely innocent, there were no guarantees. "I don't know."

AN HOUR LATER, THE SUN dipped low in the western sky. None of the law enforcement people had yet arrived on the scene, but Tab couldn't wait any longer. Nightfall came early in November, and she didn't want to ride home in the dark. It wasn't far to her grandma's house, probably only seven or eight miles, but there wasn't a clearly marked trail between here and there, and she didn't want to take a chance on getting lost.

After she gave Misty a hug, Tab made her way through the sage and dried prairie grass to where Shua was nibbling at a shrub. Aiden strode toward her. "Leaving so soon?"

"Not that it hasn't been fun," she said. "The sheriff can contact me later for a statement."

"I'm glad you're heading out while there's still enough light to see where you're going. You haven't lived around here for a couple of years. Things change."

As far as she could see, the change was minimal. The local landmarks—rolling hills, ridges and the river—were much the same as when she was a kid. On the opposite side of the Little Big Horn, she saw the sandstone cliff and the familiar arch above Half-Moon Cave. The land was eternal; the people were different.

She glanced over her shoulder at Misty's little nest on the striped wool blanket. Though Clinton had his arm around her, Misty's shoulders slumped, and her head drooped. "I'm worried about her," Tab said. "If there's anything I can do to help, call me."

"Sure."

His hand rested on Shua's neck, and he stroked along the line of the horse's mane. The gesture was completely natural, like the absentminded way you might pet a cat that jumped on your lap. This casual attitude around livestock said a lot about Aiden.

Unlike most of the men she'd dated in Billings and Missoula, he'd grown up on a ranch and was 100 percent cowboy. Right now, he was wearing a baseball cap instead of a Stetson, but he still looked the part with his long, lean body, his scuffed boots and his well-worn jeans. His hands were calloused. His wrists were strong. And his gray eyes had that cool awareness that came from hours of staring across the wide prairies, watching over several hundred head of cattle.

Had he changed? She wasn't sure.

Though she wasn't sixteen anymore, she was still a little bit blinded by her crush on him. When she looked at him, her pulse rate quickened. She had to swallow hard before she trusted herself to speak without stammering.

"I'm serious about having Misty call me," she said. "She needs a friend."

"You got that right. The girls she used to pal around with in high school are off at college, joining sororities and having all kinds of fun." A frown tugged at the corner of his mouth. "I wanted that for her. Misty's a smart kid."

"You make it sound like her life is over."

"She wanted to be a lawyer, talked about it all the time. She was planning to take on injustice and set the world straight. She'd sent off her application to a couple of universities, and she'd gotten accepted."

"A lawyer, huh? That's terrific."

"Now, she's going to be stuck on the ranch."

Tab didn't like his attitude and all that it implied. "She doesn't have to give up her dreams. Having a baby isn't the end of the world for Misty."

His gaze met hers, and she braced herself for a

bullheaded argument about how womenfolk are supposed to stay home and tend the young. Instead, Aiden said, "You're right."

"You're damn right that I'm right." She'd gotten herself all puffed up for no reason. "Right?"

"I'm not fighting you, Tab."

"Well, good."

"Misty needs to hear that she's still got opportunities. She can still go to college and to law school." His expression warmed. "It'd be good for her to spend time with you."

Being close to Misty meant also being near him, which might be the very definition of a win-win situation. She cleared her throat and reached for her saddle. "I should mount up."

"Not yet."

When he lightly touched her shoulder, she spun around to face him. He was standing so close that she could see the prisms and facets in his eyes. "What is it, Aiden?"

"If you'll wait a bit before you get up on your horse, I'd like to walk with you."

"Suit yourself."

Taking the reins, she stepped in front of Shua and made a clicking noise. The horse ambled along behind her as she and Aiden strolled along a path that followed the winding course of the river.

"To tell you the truth," he said, "I'd like to escort

you all the way back to your grandma's place and make sure you get home safely."

"I can handle myself."

"Can you? If Misty's story is true, the shooter might still be in the area."

She looked up at him. "That hadn't occurred to me."

"It's unlikely he's still around, but it's something to keep in mind. At that meeting in Crow Agency, nobody actually said we might be facing a serial killer. But it's possible."

She remembered the serious tone of the meeting and the warning to be on the lookout. "I thought the meeting was about two missing girls from Henley who were last seen on the rez."

"There's more to the story," Aiden said. "A couple of months ago, at the end of the summer, the sheriff in Billings found the body of a tourist who had been camping. She was raped and murdered. Since then, three other girls have disappeared. All the victims are blonde, like Misty."

Tab touched her long, black braid. "I guess that means I'm safe."

"You can't make that kind of assumption with a crazy person. His M.O. might change in a flash."

Fear nibbled at the edge of her mind. "I'll keep my rifle handy. And I won't dawdle."

"Call me when you get home."

Her cell phone wasn't much protection. Not

only was the reception spotty but nobody would reach her in time if she called for help. "He used Misty's rifle. Does that mean he doesn't have his own gun?"

"I don't know," Aiden said.

"Have you been working with the police? You seem to know a lot about the murdered tourist and the girls from Billings."

"I volunteer my chopper to look for missing persons, keeping an eye on things from the sky. I like to go up as often as possible."

"You enjoy flying?"

"From the first time I rode in a chopper, I loved it—swooping through the skies, leaving gravity behind and soaring free." The tension in his face relaxed as he looked heavenward and grinned. "It's the freedom. No restraints. No regrets."

"And no responsibilities," she said.

"That, too."

Aiden had been forced to take on a lot after his father died. He'd had to leave college and take care of the ranch. No wonder he wanted Misty to have a wider scope of opportunity. "I've never been in a helicopter."

"A virgin," he said.

In more ways than one, but he didn't have to know about that part of her life. "You make it sound exciting."

"It's a different perspective," he said. "I know a

lot about this territory. And that's one of the reasons I wanted to walk along with you. We might run into something along this path."

"Something?"

"Somebody," he said.

She heard a rustling in the brush beside the river and turned to look. "What is it?"

"You'll see."

A skinny man with a wild gray beard crept out from behind a tree. Over his shoulders, he wore a buffalo robe. He held a ski pole in each hand, using them as walking sticks.

"Visitors," he shouted. "Welcome, pretty lady."

Tab stood and stared. Her jaw dropped, and she felt her eyes pop wide like a cartoon version of herself. What the hell?

Chapter Four

Aiden relished the look of shock on Tab's face. It wasn't easy to ruffle her feathers, but he'd succeeded. She recovered her poise quickly. Her gaping mouth snapped shut, and her full lips smoothed into a slightly upturned line that wasn't exactly a smile. Under her breath, she muttered, "Good thing you warned me about this little *something*. I might have shot him."

No fear. Her first thought was to grab her rifle and stand ready to protect herself. He liked that attitude. This lady wasn't about to scream or take off running, not her. Not Tab.

Thinking of her as Tab instead of Tabitha was becoming easier. The longer name—Tabitha—rolled off his tongue with an almost musical resonance. Tab was one crisp, practical syllable. It suited her. The way he figured, a woman named Tab could stand up for herself while a Tabitha would be the type to flutter her eyelashes and swoon.

"Who is he?" she asked.

"His name is Wally, but everybody calls him Buffalo Man."

"Certainly not because of his size," she said. "He couldn't weigh more than one twenty-five including the fur cape and ski poles. What's he doing here?"

"He camps along the river. I spotted his tent when I did my visual sweep in the chopper."

Feet together, the scrawny gray-haired man hopped toward them, mimicking the technique of a downhill skier. Gradually, he was coming closer.

"He could be the shooter," Tab said.

"I don't reckon so. His campsite is another mile or so downriver. He was there when I flew over." Besides, Aiden had become fairly well acquainted with the old man. "He's not a murderer. A thief? Maybe. But not a killer."

Wally claimed to be part Crow, but nobody on the rez claimed him back. A drifter, he'd been in this area for three or four years. When he occasionally showed up at the Gabriel ranch looking for work, Aiden would find him something to do with the stipulation that Buffalo Man take a long soak in a hot tub and shave his whiskers. In a lucid moment, Wally had confided that he'd lost his job, his wife and his house, but he wasn't sad or self-pitying. He'd chosen to go back to nature.

Usually, he wasn't so talkative, and today he said nothing as he approached. When he was about five feet from them, Aiden caught the whiff of a powerful stench—the smell of old campfires and dirt. He held up a hand. "That's close enough, Wally."

Buffalo Man bared his yellow teeth in a grin. "That's a pretty horse."

"Thank you," Tab said. "Do you live out here?"

"It's my right. I'm Indian, like you." He cocked his head to one side. "You're Maria Spotted Bear's granddaughter."

"How do you know that?"

"I know things. Lots of things."

"You'd better not be spying on my grandma," she said. "I wouldn't like that."

He dug the tips of his ski poles into the earth and planted his fists on his skinny hips. "I am not a Peeping Tom. I have my dignity. You can ask Aiden. Go on, ask him."

"Wally does work for me at the ranch. He's a good handyman."

"Handy Wally, that's my moniker."

Aiden watched Tab's expression as her suspicion faded. It was her nature to be friendly. Her tribe had a tradition of welcoming strangers and sharing whatever they had. She took a step toward Wally and held out her hand as she offered a Crow greeting. "*Ka-hay.* My name is Tab Willows."

He vigorously shook her hand. "Pleased to meet you, Tab."

"It must get lonely out here. If you're hungry or want company, come to my grandma's house."

"I don't take charity."

"I wasn't offering," Tab said. "We'll make a trade. My grandma can use the skills of a handyman."

His yellow smile split his wizened face. Peering through his tangled mop of hair, his eyes were alert and intelligent. "I would be honored to visit the home of Maria Spotted Bear."

Though Wally had never shared his prior occupation, Aiden believed he was an educated man. His use of language was usually correct, he had a decent vocabulary and he was smart enough to know how to survive in the wild. His antisocial weirdness came from a lack of interaction with other people. He chose to be a hermit. But that didn't mean he was nuts.

"I have a couple of questions for you," Aiden said. "No doubt you noticed the commotion this afternoon."

"Gunfire. I heard it. And I saw Tab riding across the hills, coming from the east. And the chopper." He looked up at the fading light of the afternoon. "I saw your chopper. You must have seen me, too. I waved."

Aiden nodded. "What about people? Did you see or hear any people on the ground?"

Abruptly, Wally hunkered down on the ground. His voice lowered to a whisper. "After the gunfire,

I thought I should take a look and see if anybody needed my help. Voices carry a long way out here."

"Could you hear what anyone was saying?"

Wally pointed to Tab. "You. I heard you talking."

"What about earlier than that. Before Tab, did you hear voices?"

He shook his head. "I was too far away. When I got close, I heard your baby sister."

"Misty," said both Aiden and Tab.

"She laughs a lot." Wally gave a creaky chuckle of his own. "A pretty sound. Her laughter sounds like splashing water. Not like the other girls who come out here with their boyfriends. They squeal and shout and make a terrible ruckus with their parties."

Half-Moon Cave had always been a favorite gathering spot for high school parties and make-out sessions. The opening of the cave was a wide arch, similar to a band shell, and the interior provided shelter from the wind and rain. Aiden guessed that if they crossed the river and went to the cave, they'd find the remains of campfires and plenty of rusted beer cans.

"The sheriff is going to be here soon," Aiden said. "He's going to want to talk to you about what you saw or heard."

"No, sir. This is reservation land. I don't have to talk to the sheriff."

"Joseph Lefthand will be here, as well," Tab said.

"It's important to help them. There's been a murder."

"I know." Wally popped up. "I got close enough to see the dead man, and then I turned around. None of my business."

"Did you know the man who was killed?" Aiden asked.

"I might have seen him before. Once or twice. I see a lot of things. People don't much notice me." He looked directly at Tab. "Not that I go out of my way to spy on people. I mind my own business."

Aiden stepped closer to Wally and looked him straight in the eye, compelling his attention. "Bad things have been happening on or near the rez. Young girls from Henley and Billings are going missing. At least one of them was murdered. Have you seen or heard anything that could lead to the killer?"

"The man who was killed was here with a girl. She had hair like a golden waterfall."

"If you saw her photo, could you identify her?"

Wally stroked his beard and considered. "It was after dark, and I didn't really see her face. She was wearing a baby-blue sweatshirt."

That item of clothing could help identify David Welling's companion. "Did you hear them talking?"

"He said her name." Wally tugged harder on his

beard. "Ellen or Elizabeth. It was something like that."

David might have a connection with one of the missing women. And David had been murdered. If Wally stepped forward as a witness, it could put him in danger. He shouldn't be camping out here by himself.

Aiden patted him on the shoulder of his buffalo robe. "Until this is over, you might want to come and stay at the ranch. My mom has some work for you. She's going to be putting up Christmas decorations."

"I'll come after the weather gets colder," Wally said. "Right now, it's nice and warm. The river is low and slow. I go swimming in it every day. Keeps me young."

Aiden hoped Wally's outdoor skills would also keep him alive. He hated to think of anything bad happening to the eccentric old man.

AFTER TAB RETURNED TO HER grandma's house, she took care of Shua and fed the horse in the barn beside the corral. By the time she transferred her medical supplies from the saddlebags into the back of her van, the dusk had turned into dark—a still, calm night. The deep solitude soothed her. Not that she would forget the murder, the threat of a serial killer and the potential of jail time for pregnant

Misty. Tab was involved, truly involved, and she was committed to doing whatever she could to help.

But not right this minute. For now, she needed to clear her mind. She inhaled. The cold night air swept into her lungs and refreshed her mind and her spirit.

A few months ago, when she moved back here, she'd been worried that she'd be bored to death. Though the Crow half of her DNA connected her to this land and the traditions of her tribe, she'd spent most of her life in cities like Billings and Missoula where there were things to do and places to go. Not that her social life had ever been a whirlwind of parties and dates. Instead, she'd kept herself busy with her schooling and with work. After graduating from nursing school in Missoula, she'd been part of a midwife clinic that also offered prenatal and postnatal care. She'd learned so much from the other midwives.

Now, she worked alone. She was the expert.

Outside her grandma's house, she looked up at the moon and the millions of stars that spread their silvery light across the hills and distant cliffs. A couple hundred yards away, she saw the lights from other homes where the Martins and the Tall Grass families lived. The only sound was the rustling of wind across the prairies and the winged swoop of raptor birds hunting in the night.

Light shone through the windows in her grandma's kitchen where Maria Spotted Bear was probably preparing dinner and not wearing her wrist brace. Though the cast had been removed, Tab wanted Grandma Maria to protect her injured wrist until she was full strength. Twice a day, they performed therapeutic exercises. Every night, her grandma wrapped her wrist in herbal poultices. The same combination of Western medicine and Crow healing practices applied to the pills Grandma took for her heart condition.

As soon as Tab came through the front door, she heard Grandma singing in the kitchen. The stereotype of the stoic tribal elder didn't hold true for her grandma who always seemed surrounded by music and happy chatter.

Entering the kitchen, Tab saw her grandma remove a tray of cornbread from the oven. The wrist brace was nowhere in sight.

"Don't worry," Grandma said as she set the cornbread in the center of the kitchen table. "I can lift this. It's not too heavy."

"Smells good." Tab wasn't in the mood to argue. She hugged the rounded shoulders of the small woman whose long white hair was fastened at her nape with an ornately beaded barrette. "Do you know the one they call Buffalo Man?"

"A crazy old badger. He lives down by the river."

"Just to warn you, I kind of invited him to drop by anytime for dinner."

"That's my Tabitha." Her grandma chuckled. "From the time you were a little girl, you were always bringing home strays."

"His real name is Wally, and he's willing to work for his supper as a handyman. Having him drop by might be useful. The barn roof needs patching."

"How did this new friendship happen?" Grandma sat at the kitchen table. "You left the house to deliver a baby, and you picked up an old man in a buffalo robe."

"Long story."

"The stew can simmer for a while."

Not holding back, Tab told the whole story of Misty and the murder, the possible serial killer connection, the chopper and Aiden. When she mentioned his name, she heard a breathless change in her voice. She pictured the tall, lean cowboy, and a rush of excitement went through her. In an attempt to hide that reaction, she turned her back on Grandma and opened the refrigerator door to take out a pitcher of cold water.

"Aiden Gabriel," her grandma said. "He's a handsome man."

"Is he?" Her tone pitched to a higher octave. "I didn't notice. I was more concerned about his sister."

"You don't fool me. When you were a girl and spent the summer at the Gabriel ranch, you liked him, liked him very much." She sang a little song about sailing away with the man of her dreams. "Didn't you ask me for a totem to cause a man to fall in love with you?"

Tab didn't deny it. "I was a silly teenager then."

"And now, you're both grown up. Could be good timing. From what I hear, Aiden broke up with his long-time girlfriend. She lives in California and doesn't care about ranch life."

Tab poured cold spring water into a Mason jar and took a sip. People who lived on the rez seemed isolated, and yet the gossip grapevine relayed information more quickly than cell phone texting. "How do you know so much about Aiden's love life?"

"His mother and I see each other often. I bring her baked goods, and Sylvia gives me beef. She's happy about the blessing of a new baby."

"It doesn't bother her that Misty is so young and so unmarried?"

"If anyone understands about unexpected pregnancy, it's Sylvia Gabriel." Grandma leaned back in her chair and folded her hands on her lap, a signal that she was about to tell a story. "Sylvia nearly died in childbirth. She had a difficult labor, ending in Caesarian section and a serious loss of blood. But after she had Aiden, she wanted more children. She and her husband tried everything. I know this because she came to me and asked how to increase her fertility."

Maria Spotted Bear not only had a reputation as

an excellent baker but also for healing and cures. Tab had learned young how to locate, harvest and prepare many herbs for teas and salves. "Red clover, squaw berry and yams. Those are all good to promote fertility."

"Nothing worked and she gave up—satisfied to have a healthy son and a good marriage. Fourteen years later, when Sylvia was thirty-seven years old, she had Misty. A happy surprise."

Her cell phone buzzed. The screen showed Aiden was the caller. As soon as she saw his name, she remembered that she'd promised to call him when she reached her grandma's house.

"I'm home," she said when she picked up. "We're just about to sit down for dinner."

"I'm glad, but that's not why I was calling."

"Oh." She wasn't sure whether to be pleased that he trusted her to take care of herself, or to feel bad that he wasn't checking up on her.

"Misty asked if you could come over to the ranch tonight, maybe in an hour or so. Is that convenient?"

His tone was cool and distant, more appropriate for a business transaction than a personal request. "Aiden, what's going on?"

"They found another body. She's from Henley, and her name is Ellen."

That was the name Wally mentioned. He'd said that Ellen was with David Welling. "A blonde?"

"Yes."

She heard other voices in the background. They were arguing. "What else?"

"The victim was wearing a gold, engraved wristwatch. It belongs to my sister."

The link to another murder was bad for Misty. Her story about the mystery gunman who grabbed her rifle and disappeared sounded even more flimsy. Tab didn't know how she could help other than to offer moral support. Sometimes, that was enough. "I'll be there."

Chapter Five

If Tab had gotten her way, she would have tucked her grandma into bed for a solid eight hours of sleep before she left. But Grandma really wanted to come along. She argued that Sylvia Gabriel was a very good friend of the family, and friends take care of friends. What Grandma didn't say was that these murders were more exciting than anything that had happened since the fire at the casino in Crow Agency.

Sitting in the passenger seat of Tab's van, she fiddled with the wrist brace Tab had insisted that she wear. "The tribe should have jurisdiction. The dead girl was found on the rez."

Tab was tired of running through the logistical reasons why Joseph Lefthand couldn't handle a complicated investigation. She jumped to the bottom line, which was something her grandma—who took part in tribal council—would understand. "It would be expensive. The tribe would have to hire a special coroner to do the autopsies."

"Are they going to cut that poor girl open?"

Tab shot her a skeptical glance. With her long white braids, patterned wool jacket, long skirt and moccasins, Maria Spotted Bear was just a few head feathers short of playing a tribal elder at the annual reenactment of Custer's Last Stand. Not an entirely true image. Grandma kept up with the times.

"Don't pretend that you don't know about autopsies," Tab said. "You've got television on satellite dish. You've watched police shows."

"And hospital shows to keep up with what you're doing." Slyly, she asked, "Are those shows truthful?"

"Yeah, sure," Tab muttered sarcastically. "Every doctor is gorgeous, and every case is fascinating."

"You see what I mean? I've heard about detectives, but I don't know what they do."

Tab shrugged. "Neither do I. Not exactly."

"I can tell you one thing. To find a killer, you don't need fancy equipment or autopsies. You need to be smart." Grandma tapped the side of her head. "A real detective should have the instincts of a hunter."

"Do you think Joseph Lefthand has those instincts?"

"Better him than Sheriff Steve."

Tab had met both men at the meeting in Crow Agency. Both seemed decent and hard-working. Both were deeply concerned about the young women who had gone missing. Tab wondered if she ought to be more worried since she and Grandma lived alone without any security other than the rifles they kept in the front closet.

Her van jostled along the back roads between her grandma's house and the Gabriel ranch. Though Tab hadn't driven the route in years, she remembered the way. When she spent the summer at the ranch, she'd traveled back and forth many times. Later, on other visits to her grandma, she'd make a point of stopping by to see Misty…and maybe to catch a glimpse of Aiden.

"When was the last time you came to the ranch?" her grandma asked.

"It must have been two years ago. Misty was in high school." She'd been surprised by Misty's physical maturity. The little girl she'd once known had become a woman, but she'd still run to greet Tab and give her a massive hug. She hadn't seen Aiden on that trip.

Her grandma nodded. "After you moved to Missoula for nursing school, you barely had time for me on your visits."

When Tab came to her grandma's house, there was usually a specific reason, like taking care of home repairs or making sure her grandma got a checkup with the local doctor. Though Maria Spotted Bear was self-sufficient and didn't need constant watching over, both Tab and her dad made a point of checking in with Grandma, just to be sure she was okay.

As her van rounded the last curve leading to the Gabriel ranch, Tab saw lights shining from every window of the two-story, cedar-sided ranch house with the peaked roof. Several vehicles parked outside the three-car garage to the left of the house. To the right was a barn with a corrugated metal roof. She knew that Aiden lived in a separate cabin behind the barn. Did he keep his helicopter back there?

She parked her van at the end of a row of cars. From the back, she took a satchel containing a sweet potato pie and the cornbread her grandma had made for their dinner. Maria Spotted Bear never went visiting empty-handed, even though it seemed somewhat inappropriate to bring pie to a murder investigation.

Approaching the house, Tab glanced at the far left upstairs window under the eaves. That had been her bedroom during the summer she'd lived here. She remembered a long-ago night when she couldn't sleep and had perched on the sill, looking out at the long, straight driveway. She'd spotted Aiden, striding toward the house with his border collie trotting along beside him. For some reason—she'd never known why—he wasn't wearing a shirt, just his jeans, boots and hat. For a moment, he'd paused. His shoulders rose and fell as though he was sighing. He'd taken off his beat-up Stetson and tilted his head to gaze at the moon. The silvery light bathed him in an ethereal glow—an image that branded itself indelibly in her mind.

Her grandma climbed the three steps to the veranda ahead of her and rapped on the door. A stocky woman in a denim vest opened the door.

"Maria Spotted Bear," the woman said in an authoritative alto voice. "Is this an official visit? Are you representing the tribal council?"

"I'm here as Sylvia's friend," her grandma said. "This is my granddaughter, Tab Willows. Tab, this is Laura Westerfall. She's with the BIA."

Briskly, Laura shook Tab's hand. "You're the midwife. I've been meaning to pay you a visit."

"Pleased to meet you." Tab was actually more suspicious than pleased. Agents from the Bureau of Indian Affairs often caused trouble for the tribe.

"You're a trained nurse, right? And you worked with a women's clinic in Missoula."

"Have you been checking up on me?" Tab asked.

"Yes, I have. If you're planning to stay in this area, I might have a proposition for you. Recently, some grant money has come available for rural medical care, and I'd like to focus on women's health."

"On the reservation?" Tab found it hard to believe there would be any significant financial aid for the relatively small Crow population. Any money at all surprised her.

"I'm thinking of a wider area."

"So am I." The women in this wide-open country—on and off the rez—had a long way to go to reach a hospital. Many were too poor to afford decent medical care. Even the services of a midwife stretched their budgets. "Are you saying the BIA could help?"

Laura combed her fingers through her short brown hair and smiled as she held out her business card. "Give me a call. We need to talk about a women's clinic."

In spite of the current problems, Tab's spirits lifted as she imagined being able to help those who had so few resources. A grant from the BIA might be a dream come true.

Grandma interrupted her thoughts, taking the satchel with the pie and cornbread from her hands. "Where are your manners, girl? I came here to comfort Sylvia."

"In the kitchen," Laura said.

"I'll take care of her," Grandma promised. "You two should go into the living room. The boys sound like they're arguing, getting ready to lock horns."

Through an archway to the left was a paneled living room with heavy leather furniture and rugged coffee tables. In front of the moss rock fireplace, Sheriff Steve Fielding stood toe to toe with

Aiden. Since the sheriff wasn't much taller than Tab, Aiden towered over him and the two deputies he'd brought with him.

Aiden's voice was a low, dangerous growl. "I see no valid reason to take my sister into custody."

"If that's the only way you'll let me talk to her, I've got no damn choice." The sheriff waved his men into action. "Deputies, I want you to arrest—"

"Hold on." Laura inserted herself into their argument. "What's the problem, gentlemen?"

Aiden spoke first. "I wanted Sheriff Fielding to handle this investigation because I believed he was better equipped to pursue the trail of evidence in a thorough manner. Maybe I was wrong. Maybe all he wants is a quick arrest."

"You're the one who's wrong," Fielding said. "I came here to talk to Misty. Just to talk. I need some answers."

"You already took her statement."

"That cockamamie story about a mysterious shooter?"

"I won't have you harassing my sister. She's been through enough today."

Though Tab agreed that Misty shouldn't be subjected to more stress, she realized that Aiden was behaving in an unreasonable manner. And his overprotective attitude made it look like he had something to hide. "I have a compromise. What if the sheriff questions Misty while Aiden is present?"

The sheriff pointed his long, sunburned nose at her and squinted like someone who needed glasses. "You're Tab Willows, right? I need to take your statement."

"I'm happy to cooperate," she said.

"But that's not why you came here." His squint became even more pronounced. "You live with Maria Spotted Bear. Are you here to speak for your tribe?"

The politics were getting annoying. Just because Tab was half Crow, it didn't automatically make her a representative of her people. She was miles out of touch with local issues. Most of her life had been spent in Billings and Missoula. Not on the rez.

"I'm here as a concerned person," she said. "Young women are being murdered and their bodies dumped on the rez. I want to see the killer brought to justice."

"That's the voice of common sense," Laura said, backing her up. "Listen to her."

"You have no standing here, Agent Westerfall." The sheriff hitched up his belt. "You arranged for Joseph Lefthand to cede jurisdiction. This is my purview."

"Don't forget that I'm a federal agent, Sheriff. I'm not here to give orders, but I see no reason why we can't do as Tab suggested."

"Here's your reason," the sheriff said. "I can't

get the truth from Misty while she's hiding behind her big brother."

Before Aiden exploded again with righteous anger, Tab grasped his forearm and squeezed hard, compelling his attention. He wasn't helping anything by being pigheaded. She stared into his eyes. "I'll be with Misty while she's talking to the sheriff. Is that all right with both of you?"

"It's done." Laura gestured toward the hall. "Sheriff Fielding will wait down here in the office. Tab will bring Misty to talk with him immediately."

Everybody moved quickly, anxious not to destroy the fragile moment of truce. Tab found herself being escorted up the staircase by Aiden. This time, he was holding her arm above the elbow in a tight grip. His outrage manifested in a bodily heat that sizzled in the air around him.

Under his breath, he said, "I'll be damned if I let the sheriff connect Misty to these murders. He's delusional."

"Calm down." She fought to keep from being drawn into the vortex of his anger. "We have only a few minutes. Fill me in."

"The first victim was raped," he whispered.

"And the girl they just found?"

"We won't know until after the autopsy. They're transporting the body to Billings." His jaw clenched. "Usually, the sheriff would call on me for transport in the chopper. Now he's treating me like a suspect.

It's crazy. These are sex crimes. How could Misty be involved?"

On the landing at the top of the staircase, she gazed into Aiden's gray eyes, searching for the truth. "The sheriff must have a reason."

"He talked to Wally who went into detail about the wild parties he's seen up and down the river."

"Did he tell the sheriff that he saw David with a blonde girl named Ellen?"

Aiden nodded. "If Wally can be trusted, David knew the victim, but so did a lot of other people. She's a local girl. The sheriff thinks these disappearances might be a bullying thing gone wrong. When the second victim was found wearing Misty's wristwatch, he figured she was part of the gang."

Aiden had said that the sheriff wanted a quick solution, and she thought he might be right. Supposing these murders were the actions of a gang tied Welling's death to those of the missing girls. It made for a tidy solution.

She asked, "Why would he think Misty was involved?"

"She has a reputation for being wild." Aiden shook his head and looked away. "Whenever there's trouble, she seems to be the ringleader."

Tab attempted to put a positive spin on his words. "She's a leader. Headstrong. Determined."

"Great qualities if you're doing something good. And if not..." He drew in a breath and exhaled slowly. "It's not her fault. I haven't done a good job raising her."

"You're not her parent."

"Gabriel Ranch and everything that happens here is my responsibility."

He spoke with calm conviction as though his words were indisputable. When Aiden's father died, he took on that mantle. The buck stopped with him. He was the protector, the caretaker and the final authority, even though his mother had taken over the day-to-day chores and the running of the ranch.

Seeing Aiden with his head bowed made her realize that he wasn't the perfect, ideal man she'd cherished in her memories. He was real. He suffered just like any other man. Beneath his strength was a thick layer of sadness. He'd given up everything for his family. Somehow, that made him even more attractive to her. She wanted to comfort him and tell him that everything was going to be all right.

"Let me handle the sheriff," she said. "If Misty is under too much stress, I'll call an end to the questioning."

He looked doubtful. "What if—"

"Stop," she said quietly. "There's only one thing that needs to happen. Misty has to tell the truth."

"That's what scares me."

His fear touched her.

Though it seemed impossible, Misty could be involved in these dark, terrible crimes. Tab didn't want to believe it was possible.

Chapter Six

In the downstairs office at the ranch, the decor showed a more feminine touch than the rest of the house. Sylvia spent most of her time behind the polished-oak desk, surrounded by antique wooden filing cabinets. A jar of jelly beans sat at the corner of the desk beside a bowl of fresh yellow roses. The computer screen saver showed a Degas painting of ballet dancers.

Sheriff Fielding perched on the edge of the desk facing Tab and Misty who were at opposite ends of a blue love seat. From what Aiden had told her, Tab knew that the sheriff considered Misty to be a prime suspect. But she saw hesitation and doubt in his eyes.

With a flannel robe belted above her pregnant belly, Misty couldn't have looked less like the ringleader of a murderous gang. Under the pink velour robe, she wore striped yellow pajamas. Her freshly washed hair piled on top of her head with wispy blond curls escaping to frame her face. Her eyes were red-rimmed as though she'd been crying.

The sheriff cleared his throat. "Misty, it's very important for you to be honest with me and tell me everything, even if you think it might get somebody else in trouble. This isn't like high school. People are getting killed."

"I know," Misty said. "I saw David die."

"Do you know Ellen Jessop?" the sheriff asked.

"Is she…is she dead?"

"I'm asking the questions, young lady." His voice took on an authoritative edge. "Were you and Ellen friends?"

"We were both cheerleaders, but she's a year older than me. Oh God, this is awful. The last time I saw her, we argued."

"About what?"

Fidgeting on the sofa, she plucked apart a tissue she clutched in her hand. "I don't want to say."

Tab reached over and placed her hand on Misty's arm. "You need to cooperate. Tell us about Ellen."

"We were never really good friends. She used to date Clinton, and she hated that he was the father of my baby. She said that the only reason Clinton was with me instead of her was because my family is rich."

Tab watched as the sheriff nodded. Had he heard this story before? In a small town like Henley, word traveled fast.

Misty continued, "Ellen's family was going through hard times. After she graduated high school, they couldn't afford to send her to college, and she had to work at the Feed and Seed store in Henley."

"When was the last time you saw her?" Tab asked gently.

"About a month ago. She was coming out of the drugstore, and I was going in. She asked me what time it was because she was late for work." Misty giggled, and then frowned. "She said work was something I'd never had to think about, and she made it sound like I didn't have a care in the world. But I do."

The sheriff cleared his throat. "What did you say to her?"

"Everybody thinks my life is a breeze, but it's not." Her small fist clenched. "I'm having a baby. That's going to be hard, really hard. Why don't other people understand? All they see is money. They think being rich makes everything right."

"It helps," the sheriff said.

Misty lifted her chin. "I'd burn every dollar if I could have my daddy back. That's what I really want. People are all that matters. I miss my daddy. Every day, I miss him."

"I'm sorry for your loss," the sheriff said.

His perfunctory tone made Tab think that his former empathy was fading fast. In this part of the world, people assumed that Misty Gabriel was a pretty, rich girl without a care. Tab knew better— she remembered the seven-year-old who tried to make everyone happy with the sound of her laughter while she cried herself to sleep every night.

The sheriff leaned forward. "Let's get back to what happened when you saw Ellen for the last time."

"I told her the time, and she made a snotty comment about my solid gold wristwatch. It made me mad. I took off the watch and threw it at her. Then I walked away."

"Did you try to get your watch back?" the sheriff asked.

"I wanted to. Aiden gave it to me on my sweet sixteen, and he had it engraved with my name and birth date. I meant to call Ellen, but I never did."

Her explanation sounded plausible—childish but believable. And yet, Tab sensed that Misty was holding something back. There was more to the story of the wristwatch. "Is there anything else you want to say?"

Misty refused to meet her gaze. Instead, she giggled and placed her hands on her belly. "The baby is kicking, really hard. I think it's a girl, a dancer."

Was she being deliberately evasive? Sheriff Fielding seemed to think so. His attitude toward Misty turned more hostile. "Tell me about the party at Heather Gardener's house last weekend."

"I didn't go. Parties aren't much fun when you're pregnant and you can't drink and you dance like an elephant." After another giggle, she asked, "Who told you I went to that party?"

Though the sheriff said nothing, Misty's eyes narrowed as she stared at him. "I know who it was," she said. "Your deputy's daughter. Christina? It was her, wasn't it? She told you I went to the party. But she's mistaken. I wasn't there."

"What about Clinton? Did he go by himself?"

"I don't know." With an effort, she pushed herself to her feet. "Are we done here?"

"Not yet," the sheriff said.

Tab fully expected Misty to win this standoff. Sheriff Fielding might have the law on his side, but Misty was a stubborn, pregnant woman with the power of rampaging hormones. Hoping to mediate, Tab stood. "Sheriff, it might be time for us to take a break. You still need to take my statement."

"I have more questions for Misty."

"No," Misty said as tears spurted from her eyes. "There isn't anything else to say. I just can't—"

From outside the house, gunfire exploded. Tab heard loud whoops and several shots as though two or more guns were being fired. In an instant, the atmosphere inside the house shifted from simmering hostility to a fierce, boiling anger. She heard people running, shouting, gathering their weapons and preparing to defend their property.

Whether the sheriff liked it or not, this interview was over.

AT THE SOUND OF SHOTS being fired, Aiden dashed from the kitchen where he'd been having sweet potato pie and tea with his mom and Maria Spotted Bear. In the front entryway, he saw both deputies peering through the window by the front door with their handguns drawn. They signaled for him to stay back.

Like hell, he would. In his house, Aiden gave the orders.

The ranch foreman, Blake Henry, pushed the front door open. "They're gone. The gunfire came from a pickup truck. They threw something and took off, heading south."

"Did you get a license plate?" a deputy asked.

"I barely had time to see the truck," Blake drawled. "If you drive like fury, you might catch them."

The sheriff stalked down the hallway from the office. "You heard him. Go."

Aiden knew the deputies didn't have a chance of catching up with a speeding truck. It was only about seven miles to an intersection where the paved county road led to Henley in less than ten miles. Though the sheriff already had his cell phone out, he didn't have enough manpower to set up an effective traffic net in a matter of minutes.

A crowd spilled into the front entryway. His mom and Maria Spotted Bear came from the kitchen. Two other ranch hands entered through the front door. Misty and Tab followed the sheriff down the hall. There wasn't time for Aiden to discuss his plan with the whole group. He knew what was needed, and he intended to do it. Pivoting on his heel, he bolted through the front door.

Anger pounded through his veins as he ran across the yard and past the barn. His home and family had been endangered. Shots were fired at his house, and he'd be damned if he let anyone get away with that kind of threat.

Behind his cabin, his chopper stood ready and waiting. As he flung open the door to the cockpit, he heard a shout.

"Wait for me."

"Tab?" What the hell was she doing here?

"Don't waste time talking. I'm coming with you."

There wasn't time to argue. He helped her into the cockpit where she dove into the copilot seat and fastened her belt. He hit the starter, throttled back and took off. Over the roar of the rotors, he heard Tab yelling as they swooped across the darkened landscape.

A quick glance told him that she wasn't screaming in fear. The lights from the instrument panel reflected the excitement in her big, beautiful blue eyes. Her mouth opened wide in the biggest grin he'd ever seen on her face.

"Headset," he said as he pointed to the equipment. "Put it on."

After a bit of fumbling, she got the headset on and activated so they could talk to each other.

"This is great," she said. "I know we have something else to be thinking about, but this is just so much fun."

"Why did you come after me?"

She leaned toward the windshield and peered into the night. "I had a pretty good idea about what you were doing, and I wanted to help."

"To help," he said. "How?"

"I'm a second pair of eyes. We're looking for a truck, right?"

Instead of discussing her plan, she'd acted on instinct, which was exactly what he'd done. He shouldn't be mad at her for that, but he sure as hell didn't need her help. Taking care of problems was what he did. He maneuvered the chopper until the graded gravel road leading to the house was beneath them, and then he turned on the wide-angle searchlight.

"How did you keep up with me?" he asked. "I was running."

"You're wearing stiff-soled boots," she pointed out. "I'm in sneakers. Plus, I'm pretty speedy."

"Is that so?" Her smile was adorable, but he refused to be charmed. As far as he was concerned, she'd stuck her pretty little nose into his family business. Misty might need the kind of comfort that Tab could offer, but he worked alone.

"The derivation of *Tabitha* is gazelle," she said. "And *Aiden* is fire."

Why did she know the meaning of his name? There was something going on here that he didn't understand. "Fire, huh?"

"It suits you. You're a fiery type."

"And you're fast."

"On my feet, I'm fast. In other ways, you can call me molasses." She pointed through the window. "There's the deputy's car with the lights flashing."

The truck was nowhere in sight, and they were almost to the county road. Aiden concentrated on piloting the chopper. They were flying low at high speed. For anyone else, this would have been a dangerous move. At night, the low-hanging power lines and high branches of trees were nearly invisible. But this was his territory. He knew when to zig and when to zag. "I think I'll go left toward Henley."

"Good plan," she said. "If we don't see them by the time we get to town, we can double back."

He aimed the searchlight on the road and surged forward. A mile down the road to Henley, he spotted the truck.

"There they are," Tab said. "Now what do we do?"

"If I were alone, I'd drop down and buzz the truck until they drove off the road. But I don't want to draw their fire with you sitting in the copilot's seat."

"Well, then. It's a good thing I came along."

Not if the truck got away while he was playing it safe. He didn't want these guys to get all the way into town where they could crawl into a hole and hide. "We're going to set up an ambush."

His plan was to get ahead of the truck and set the chopper down in the middle of the road. The truck would have to hit the brakes. When they stopped, he'd shoot out their tires. There wasn't time to explain all that to Tab.

"When I touch down," he said, "you jump out and run. Take cover. Understand?"

"Got it."

He zoomed ahead and set the chopper down in the middle of the road. In the distance, he could see the headlights of the truck approaching. Reaching behind his seat, he grabbed his rifle.

From the corner of his eye, he saw Tab throw off her seat belt and climb out. She hit the ground running, just like he'd told her. There wasn't a lot of cover nearby, but she found a couple of granite rocks and ducked behind them. He followed her.

Beside her, he went up on one knee and took aim.

The truck came to a stop.

Before Aiden could fire, both doors on the cab

swung open and a couple of guys jumped out. Their hands were raised over their heads.

"Don't shoot." Both men were yelling. "We surrender. Don't shoot."

Aiden's trigger finger itched. He would have liked to blast the tires and put a couple of holes in the doors of the truck just to teach these guys a lesson. But he didn't want to give them a reason to press charges against him for destroying their property.

"Tab, you stay put." He stood with his rifle still held at the ready. "This might be a trap."

"Could be somebody else in the back of the truck," she said. "Be careful."

Walking toward them, he yelled, "On your knees. Hands locked behind your head."

Quickly, they followed his order. As he approached, he could see the fear in their eyes. They were young, not much older than Misty. One of them wore a beat-up Denver Broncos cap and an oversize jersey with the number fifteen celebrating Tebow, the former quarterback who pulled off a couple of miracle wins. The other appeared to be part Crow.

After he checked the bed of the truck and was satisfied that nobody else was hiding amid the junk that had accumulated there, he took a position in front of the young men. Aiden didn't lower his rifle.

"Where are your guns?" he demanded.

"In the truck," said the Bronco fan. "We didn't mean any harm. We fired into the air to get your attention."

"Nobody threatens my home." Aiden was dead serious. "If you have a problem, you come to me. Like a man."

"Yes, sir."

"Give me your names."

"I'm Woody Silas." He wore the Bronco cap. "And this here is Chuck Longbeak."

Aiden heard Tab come up behind him. "Longbeak," she said. "I know your sister."

His dark eyes pleaded. "You can't tell my sister. She'll tell my mom."

"Your mom will know," Tab said. "You boys are about to get yourselves arrested. The deputies are already on their way."

"We didn't do nothing wrong," Woody said. He was almost crying. If this was an act, it was a good one. "We just flung something in your driveway and fired into the air."

"You broke plenty of laws," Aiden said. "You fled a police officer. You were speeding. You did malicious mischief. If I really pushed, that mischief charge might get upgraded to assault with a deadly weapon."

"Nobody got hurt," Woody yelped.

"What did you throw into my driveway?"

The two young men exchanged a nervous glance.

This time it was Chuck Longbeak who did the talking. "We wrapped up a note inside a hunting magazine so it would have some heft. Woody threw it. He's got a good arm. He was a quarterback."

"What did the note say?" Tab asked.

Chuck buttoned his lip. He was acting like this was nothing but a harmless prank, and Aiden was running short on patience. "Answer the lady."

"David Welling was my friend," Chuck said. "He got me a job with his uncle at the gas station. I liked David. He shouldn't be dead."

"His death," Tab said, "saddens us all. David should have had many more years."

Chuck turned his head to glare at Aiden. "It's your sister's fault. He loved her. And she shot him."

He spoke with the kind of assurance that came from knowing what had happened, almost as though he'd been there at the time of the shooting. "How do you know? Were you there?"

"No." Chuck shook his head. They both looked guilty as hell. Something else was going on with them.

"But you know the area. You know where David got shot." Aiden paused. "I'm going to ask you again. Think hard and tell me the truth. Were you there?"

"Not this time."

His answer implied that there had been other times. "It wasn't sheer dumb luck that David ended up in a place where my sister was. He must have been following her."

Woody spoke up, "We don't know nothing about that."

"I think you do," Aiden pressed. "I think you were all spying on Misty, keeping an eye on her. How many times did you drive by the ranch, looking for her?"

"Maybe once or twice," Chuck admitted.

"Shut up," Woody growled. "We don't have to tell him that. He's not a cop."

"I'm going to let you in on a little secret, kid. I'm a man with a gun. That means I ask the questions and you give the answers."

Chuck lifted his chin. "I only know one thing for sure. David loved Misty, and she broke his heart."

"What did the note say?"

Chuck mumbled, "It's your fault, Misty. You killed him. His death is on your hands."

Aiden heard the deputy's sirens getting closer. He'd be glad to turn these two over to the law, not that he thought any of the charges would stick. Woody and Chuck represented the tip of the iceberg. Lots of townspeople would be quick to blame Misty, whether or not she was guilty.

Chapter Seven

From the copilot seat, Tab looked down at the road. The chopper hovered high enough that the wind from the rotors didn't churn up the dirt and dead leaves on the ground. She watched the deputies slap the cuffs on Chuck and Woody. While one of them kept an eye on the boys, the other gathered the guns from Woody's truck, moved their vehicle to the side of the road and slapped a police sticker on the door.

Beside her, Aiden said nothing. She had the impression that he was annoyed with her but didn't know why. The more she got to know him, the harder he was to understand. Life had been a lot simpler when she'd simply admired him from afar. Ten years ago, she'd thought he was perfect. Now? Not so much.

Reality had no place in idealized love. What did the poets call it? Unrequited love—a gut-churning passion, an obsession that was totally one-sided, like the feelings David must have had for Misty.

From what Tab knew, poor David Welling didn't really know the object of his affection. He hadn't spent enough time with Misty to be irritated by her giggle or to see her when she didn't look her best.

People did crazy things in the throes of unrequited love. When Tab had her teenage crush, she'd pined away her entire summer at the Gabriel ranch without dating, not that there had been a lot of guys asking. Only two, and she had turned both down. She'd been saving her heart for the man of her dreams, the twenty-one-year-old Aiden who barely knew she existed in spite of the way she continually arranged to accidentally on purpose run into him. When he mentioned that green was his favorite color, she'd worn her one green T-shirt for three days in a row. Plus green eyeshadow. And green ribbons in her hair. *Crazy.*

What kinds of things had David done?

The possibilities made her shudder.

One thing seemed certain. His unrequited love for Misty made his murder less random. He was watching her. The fact that he'd turned up in the middle of nowhere to help Misty when the Jeep got stuck wasn't a coincidence.

Tab glanced at Aiden and spoke into the microphone on her headset. "Do you think David was following Misty and Clinton?"

"I do," he said tersely.

"Because he was in love."

"Or stalking her."

Below, she saw the deputies load the two law-breakers into the back of their car and drive toward Henley. The boys would spend the night in the local jail, which would give them time to think. Would they change their minds about Misty? She doubted it.

As the chopper swept into motion, she spoke again, hoping to melt the glacier that had formed between her and Aiden. "I guess the whole town knows about David's murder."

"And they've already decided that Misty is guilty."

"A hasty conclusion."

"People are like that. They want answers."

"But there hasn't been an investigation. The sheriff hasn't even taken my statement, and I'm the closest thing he has to an eye witness."

"There's evidence," he reminded her. "Unfortunate evidence. Ballistics will show that Misty's rifle fired the shot that killed David. Her fingerprints are on the gun, and she admitted firing it. That might be all the proof the sheriff needs to arrest her."

That was the most talking he'd done since she got into the chopper with him. "Evidence might be fact. But it isn't necessarily the truth."

"My sister isn't a killer."

"I know." He had absolutely no call to make that statement; she hadn't once accused Misty. Still, she supposed he was under stress and she ought to cut him some slack. "Don't worry. We'll find the truth. Even if we have to do our own investigation, we'll find the killer."

"That's not going to happen, Tab. We aren't going to run around playing detective."

She wasn't sure if he was rejecting the idea of investigating or rejecting her personally. "You don't seem too pleased with the way Sheriff Fielding is handling things."

"I'm not."

"And I'm not suggesting that we get in the sheriff's way. But I don't see any reason why we shouldn't do some poking around on our own."

"I like you." He turned his head to look directly at her. "I'd like to get to know you better...but not like this. Protecting my family isn't your problem."

He was beginning to tick her off. "Because you don't think I can handle it?"

"I didn't say that."

"You know, Aiden, you're the one who called me and asked me to come to the ranch."

"Because Misty needed you."

"And you don't."

"Correct."

Waves of arrogance radiated from him. "I just want to help. Don't be so quick to turn your back."

Contradictory feelings braided into a knot that tightened in her belly. She ought to be elated because he wanted to spend time with her, but he was pushing her away at the same time.

"You're angry," he said.

"Confused."

"I don't want to put you in danger. There's a serial killer out there."

"Right," she said. "And I want to help catch him. You don't always have to do everything by yourself."

Though he nodded, she didn't really think he got her point. Why couldn't he understand? Nobody was meant to go it alone, not even a man like Aiden who had taken on big responsibilities when his father died. There was no shame in accepting help.

"I'm going to make you smile again," he said. "Get ready."

"You're trying to change the subject."

"Maybe."

He slowed the forward speed until they were standing still, poised on a current of air. Aiden adjusted the gears, and the chopper made a rapid ascent as though they were riding an invisible elevator. The land below them faded away. Higher and higher, they lifted into the night sky, and then they stopped.

With the flick of a couple of switches, he turned off the running lights and the lights in the cockpit. Suspended in the velvet darkness, she experienced a strange, almost magical sensation. The stars closed around her and she became part of the sky. She could feel the altitude. The only reminder of reality was the synchronized rumble of the rotors. Looking down, she saw dots of light from ranch houses and a warmer glow from the streets of Henley, miles from where they were.

"Do you like it?" he asked.

Though she hadn't been aware of holding her breath, she exhaled in a whoosh. "I feel like the wind, a feather on the wind."

"You're not a helicopter virgin anymore."

"I understand why you love flying. It's so free."

"Up here, I can leave the worries behind. But only for a couple of minutes." He turned on the lights and set a course for home. "Usually when I'm up in the chopper, I'm on my way to a disaster. A rescue. A search. A medical emergency."

She closed her eyes, not wanting to come down to earth. Her memory bank made a permanent record of these magical moments with Aiden. "Thank you."

"Am I forgiven?"

"Not entirely," she said, "but mostly. And do you forgive me for coming with you without permission?"

"You bet," he said. "I'm wondering if you told anybody else your plan before you took off running after me."

"I told Grandma, and she was pleased." Come

to think of it, her reaction was kind of odd. "She said something about how I was meant to be with you, whatever that means."

To her surprise, he chuckled. "This might be a good time to warn you about your grandma and my mom. I was with them in the kitchen while the sheriff was talking to you and Misty. And the two of them were plotting."

"About what?"

"Matchmaking," he said.

"Between you and me?" Though she'd been making that same match ever since she saw him, Tab didn't like being manipulated. "Why do you think so?"

"They kept winking and nudging each other. Then my mom announced that you didn't have a boyfriend and wasn't that convenient because I don't have a girlfriend, either."

"Subtle," Tab muttered.

"When I said I liked the sweet potato pie, your grandma told me that you made it."

"Why would she say that?"

"To let me know that you're a great cook."

Tab groaned. Of course, her grandma would push the anatomically incorrect old wives' tale about the way to a man's heart being through his stomach. "Does that turn you on? Thinking that I know my way around a kitchen?"

"Do you?"

"As a matter of fact, I'm fully capable of making a pie, but I didn't make that one. There wasn't time after I got back to Grandma's, took care of Shua and drove to your ranch."

"Busy day."

Running through the short list of what she'd done in one day made her aware of the time. Her wristwatch showed it was after ten o'clock. She should have been tired, but she wasn't. A restless energy coursed through her. No doubt, she was still feeling the effect of the adrenaline rush that came from flying and from being this close to Aiden.

As they approached the ranch, he turned on the searchlight and scanned the landing area behind the barn. Looking down on his cabin, she noticed a deck that was half the size of the house, a good place for a barbecue. "When did you build the cabin?"

"A couple of summers ago. I wanted to put some space between me and the main house. My mom and Blake—he's the foreman—are handling most of the ranch business. If I'm not around, they don't come running to me."

Apparently, he needed to physically move to avoid taking over. "And the separate cabin gives you some privacy."

"Mom and Blake are the ones who need space of their own. They still sleep in separate bedrooms, but they've been a couple for quite a while."

"Does that bother you?"

"Hell, no. I want my mom to be happy. Her life didn't end when my father died. It took her a long time to crawl out of her depression. When she did, Blake was there, waiting to give her a hand."

The chopper touched down, and the rotors stilled. Without that noise, the night seemed uncomfortably quiet. Tab wasn't sure where to go from here. "It's late," she said.

"You and your grandma should stay at the ranch tonight. We've got plenty of room."

Suspiciously, she asked, "Did you think of that invitation all by yourself? Or is it something your mom and my grandma suggested?"

"Both," he said. "About the matchmaking…"

"What about it?"

"I'm not opposed."

When she emerged from the chopper and set her feet on hard ground, her legs were shaky. After flying, the earth felt too solid and heavy. She circled the tail and stood beside Aiden. "When you say you aren't opposed, I'm not sure what that means. Are you asking me on a date?"

"I'm asking you to spend the night."

She avoided looking at him. His offer to stay the night hadn't been meant in a romantic way, and she didn't want to react like a moron. "Normally, I wouldn't impose, but this is a long day for Grandma. She needs her sleep."

"And so do you."

His low, sexy voice caressed her senses. Quickly, she said, "And I'm concerned about Misty. All this stress while she's pregnant isn't good for her."

"Look at me, Tab."

With great reluctance, she lifted her gaze. With the moonlight shining on his face, he reminded her of that iconic image of the perfect man she'd seen on that night so long ago when he was walking his dog. "Whatever happened to Reilly?"

"My border collie? Oh, man, I loved that dog." His mouth relaxed into a smile. "I miss good old Reilly. He died last year and I buried him up on the hill. Why do you ask?"

She really couldn't say. Standing this close to him had turned her into a tongue-tied sixteen-year-old with a heartrending crush. "I don't know."

With the back of his hand, he smoothed a wisp of hair off her cheek. "We've been through a lot together, Tab. But I hardly know you."

Her chin tilted upward. The intense focus of his gray eyes warmed her. A trembling heat rippled through her body. "What do you want to know?"

His hand nestled on the nape of her neck under her braid, and he held her in place. When he leaned closer, she knew he was about to kiss her, and the anticipation was almost more than she could stand. Her knees turned to jelly. For years, she'd dreamed of this moment.

His lips touched hers. The light pressure intoxi-
cated her. *This is it.* This moment was something
she'd waited for and imagined and cherished. She
wanted more, and she couldn't hold back. Her level
of excitement surged off the charts, and her heart
raced madly. If she'd been hooked to a monitor,
the machine would have exploded. She pressed her
mouth harder against his. Their gentle kiss became
fierce and passionate.

Her arm flung around his neck. Her body molded
to his. She wanted to feel him in every fiber of
her being. His arm snuggled around her waist and
yanked her so tightly against him that her breasts
crushed against his hard-muscled chest.

This kiss was as wonderful as she had imagined. Better, it was better because it was real and
not the fantasy of a lovesick girl. In his arms, she
was a woman.

Gasping, she ended the kiss and tucked her head
into the crook of his neck. When her eyes closed, a
tear squeezed through her lashes and slipped down
her cheek.

"I'll stay the night," she whispered.

Tonight and tomorrow and the next day, she
wanted to stay with him, even if it meant she might
get hurt. Some risks were worth the pain.

Chapter Eight

As they walked toward the house, Aiden's mind was a thousand miles away. His instincts told him to fling Tab over his shoulder, carry her back to his cabin and make love to her real slow. The rational side of his mind reined him back. Too soon, it was too soon. He probably shouldn't have kissed her in the first place, but he was glad he did. For a woman who acted so professional, she sure as hell had a wild side and a sexy energy that bowled him over. That wasn't a friendly little kiss. It was foreplay.

"Aiden," she said, "are you listening?"

"I drifted off for a moment." He shook off his fantasies and dismissed the image of her lying in her bed with her long black hair spread across the pillows. "You were saying?"

"When Misty was talking to the sheriff about her wristwatch, she was holding something back."

"She was lying?"

"Not lying, but not telling everything. It had something to do with a party."

With an effort, he tamped down his desire. "I gave her that pretty gold watch, and I thought it meant something to her. I'm surprised she lost it."

"She didn't misplace it," Tab said. "She argued with the girl who was murdered, Ellen Jessop, and ended up throwing the watch at her."

Pitching a tantrum sounded exactly like something Misty would do. Not only did she have a temper but she often acted in haste without considering the consequences. "Did she ask for the watch back?"

"Not according to her."

Approaching the wide porch that stretched across the front of the house, he noticed that the sheriff's vehicle was still there. "I'm guessing that the sheriff talked to her while we were gone. She's got to tell the truth, but I hope that being honest won't get her deeper in trouble."

"It won't," Tab said emphatically. "She's innocent."

"I'll talk to her." He glanced up at Misty's second-floor bedroom window at the far right end of the house. The lights were still on. "Looks like she's still awake. I'll catch her before she goes to sleep."

"I have a question," she said. "Does Clinton stay here with Misty?"

"No." Aiden had laid down the law on this topic.

"Unless they get married, Clinton doesn't live here."

"Well, aren't you the old-fashioned one."

"I don't have a problem with Clinton visiting and even spending the night, but there's a commitment that comes with having a baby, and they both need to step up, make plans and act like grown-ups."

"Does he have a job?"

"My mom hired him." He didn't like that arrangement, but the economy was tough, and Clinton hadn't been able to find other employment. "But he doesn't stay in the bunkhouse. He lives in Henley with his parents. The Browns are good folks, and they agree with me."

"But how does Misty feel about the arrangement?"

Most of his sister's feelings and attitudes were incomprehensible to him. She'd laugh when she ought to cry. She could handle a big trauma but would blow up over breaking a heel on her shoe. "I think she gets it. There's a reason she hasn't married Clinton, and it's not because he hasn't asked. He did the honorable thing and came to me for permission."

"Another old-time tradition," she said. "Is the Gabriel ranch in some kind of time warp?"

"Would that be such a bad thing?"

"Not for you," she said. "For someone like me, it's a different story. I'm half Crow and half white.

I'm pretty sure I wouldn't fare well in the Old West."

"A beautiful woman like you always has an advantage."

"Thanks, but—" with a flick of her slender wrist, she brushed his compliment aside "—there's a lot more expected from a modern woman than being pretty. What's it going to take for me to drag you into this century?"

"Go ahead." He grinned. "You can try to change my mind."

"Challenge accepted."

They stepped onto the porch, and he made a point of opening the door for her. There was nothing wrong with his supposedly old-fashioned view of life. His father, his grandfather and his great-grandfather had raised cattle on this land, built a small empire and made a good life for their families. Not a damn thing wrong with that.

In the front room, the sheriff paced with his cell phone to his ear, still irritated and hostile. Misty occupied a big leather chair near the fireplace with her feet in fuzzy slippers up on an ottoman. His mom and Blake were opposite her on the love seat.

His mom rose and came toward them. She took Tab's hands and smiled. "Maria was exhausted. I told her to go to bed."

"I appreciate that, Sylvia. Grandma needs her sleep."

"Come here." Sylvia pulled her into a warm hug. "There hasn't been time for us to say a proper hello. I'm so glad to see you."

"Same here."

Over his mom's shoulder, Tab gave him a wink. He wondered how long it would take for his mom to start fitting her for a wedding gown. For a woman so dead set on matchmaking, his mom was doing a good job of holding Blake at bay. Tab had included him in her hugging, and they resembled the beginnings of one big happy family.

He couldn't join in, not yet. Aiden had a job to do. He needed to mend fences with Sheriff Fielding who had just ended his phone call. Like it or not, the sheriff was his best source of information.

Aiden cleared his throat. "Your deputies did a fine job in arresting those two. They were thorough."

"Did you expect anything less?"

"You know how much I respect you and your men." And that was the genuine truth. More than once, the idea of becoming a lawman had crossed his mind. "We've worked together on rescues and searches. I've never turned my back when you've asked for help, and I hope we can continue with that kind of cooperation."

The sheriff nodded slowly. "Apology accepted."

Aiden hadn't actually humbled himself enough to ask for forgiveness. *Real men never say they're sorry.* He winced a little bit as he realized that was probably another example of his old-fashioned thinking. But it worked. He and the sheriff were back on the same page and he was free to ask, "What was in that note the boys threw at the house?"

"They wrote it in crayon on a piece of notebook paper," Sheriff Fielding said with obvious disgust. "Real childish. Real stupid."

Misty piped up, "I saw the note. My name was scribbled, all mean and nasty, and it said David's death was on my head."

He glanced toward his sister. Usually, she liked being the center of attention, but not like this. Her eyelids drooped. Her skin was pale. "Are you okay?"

"I'm tired."

While Tab and his mother rushed to Misty's side, Aiden lowered his voice to speak to the sheriff. "Is this the kind of nonsense you expect from Chuck and Woody?"

"They've both got juvenile records. Nothing serious."

"They claimed that they were just shooting in the air, but I want some serious charges so they understand that gunfire of any kind isn't acceptable."

"I agree," the sheriff said. "That prank could have turned dangerous."

The sheriff had been looking for a gang, and now he had the start of one with Woody and Chuck.

Aiden wanted more information, but he didn't expect the sheriff to be forthcoming in front of the other people in the room, especially Misty. He nodded toward the kitchen. "Sheriff, you look like you could use some coffee."

"If I have caffeine at this hour, I'll never get to sleep."

"A beer?"

"I wouldn't say no to a cup of tea."

His mom caught the reference to beverages and was already moving toward them. Aiden gestured for her to step back. "I'll make the tea. You take care of Misty."

In the kitchen, he set the teakettle on the burner and sat at the table opposite the sheriff. "Earlier tonight, you said that you suspected the murders might be the work of a gang. Are there any other guys that Chuck and Woody hang out with?"

"All these kids pal around together. Like Wally the Buffalo Man said, they get together for parties and make a ruckus. They can get away with a lot as long as they don't cause a disturbance in town."

"So they go to the rez."

"I guess they do. Two and a half million acres of land that's mostly unsupervised is real tempting."

"Is there anyone who stands out?" Aiden asked. "A leader of the pack."

"I've been keeping my eye on a guy who's only been in town for six months or so. He's older than these kids, probably twenty-six or twenty-seven, and a ski bum type. They call him Aspen Jim. His last name is Sherman."

"Where does he work?"

"At the feed store. He must have known the girl who got murdered. She worked there, too."

The teakettle gave a whistle, and Aiden put together a couple of mugs with tea bags and sugar. His natural inclination was to ask direct questions and expect answers, but he was still on thin ice with the sheriff and needed to be cautious. "I hope you don't mind if I ask about your investigation."

"Let's just keep in mind that this is my investigation. *Mine*, not yours." The sheriff raised his mug and took a sip of the hot tea. "And there are some things I can't tell you. After all, your sister is a suspect."

"I understand."

Aiden was counting on the years of goodwill his family had established with the people in these parts. The Gabriel ranch was a big employer, his mom attended church regularly, and Aiden had the reputation of being fair and honest. To keep Misty out of jail, he might need to call in a whole lot of favors.

"Tell you what," the sheriff said, "you go ahead and ask your questions. If I need to hold back, I'll tell you."

"Fair enough." He gave a nod. "When do you

think you'll get those autopsy reports back from Billings?"

"A couple of days," he said. "They put a rush on it. If we've got a serial killer dumping bodies on the rez, we need to know."

Joseph Lefthand had strongly suggested that possibility at the meeting in Crow Agency. He'd warned people in law enforcement to be on the lookout. "What can you tell me about Ellen Jessop's murder?"

"Her body was found in a gully not far from where Spring Creek Road takes a jog. I wouldn't mind if you happened to fly over with your chopper. You might be able to see something that the guys on the ground missed."

Aiden nodded. "If I see anything, I'll report to you."

"Ellen's death might not be related to David's, but it's hard not to put the two together. Not that Wally is a reliable witness, but he said that he saw David with Ellen."

"What can you tell me about the other murdered girl?"

"Raped." The sheriff winced as he sipped his tea. "Bruising showed she'd been beaten, and the cause of death was manual strangulation. She'd been restrained. When they found the body, her wrists were still tied together."

"What kind of knots?"

"Nothing special," the sheriff said, "figure eight knots and bowlines. Sailors use those knots, but so do cowboys."

"No DNA or fingerprints?"

"Nothing." The sheriff finished off his tea and pushed back his chair to stand. "I'm about done here. Before I go, I'd like to take Tab's statement."

"She'll be relieved to give it to you."

"I remember her from way back. She was a skinny little thing, but when she looked at you with those blue eyes, she'd make you stop and stare. She's grown into a pretty woman."

"I won't disagree," Aiden said. She was most definitely a pretty woman, and she kissed like there was no tomorrow.

"Smart, too. We could use a professional mid-wife in these parts. I sure hope she decides to stick around."

Aiden intended to do everything in his power to convince her to stay. This was the place she belonged, the place she would learn to call home.

BRIGHT AND EARLY THE next morning, Tab took her coffee mug onto the porch and perched on the railing facing her grandma who had settled into a rocking chair. A relaxed smile stretched across Grandma's lined and weathered face. She reminded Tab of Yoda or the Native American version of

Buddha—an icon of wisdom, strength and happiness.

If she told her grandma about the kiss last night, she wondered what Maria Spotted Bear would advise her to do. Should she play hard to get? Should she flirt? Or should she shamelessly throw herself at him? Seeing Aiden this morning could be complicated.

"It's a beautiful day," Tab said. Not a cloud in sight, the newly risen sun illuminated the big blue Montana sky. Flying in daylight would be a new experience, one she was anxious to try.

"Not too cold," Grandma said as she sipped from her own steaming mug. "It's a good November."

Tab savored the rich, fragrant coffee. Since her grandma preferred tea, she seldom indulged the coffee habit she'd developed in Missoula when working late nights with women in labor. "Are you ready to head for home?"

"Not so fast. Let me drink my coffee."

"Really? You're not having tea?"

"Sylvia adds a pinch of wild chicory root for me. It's good for digestion. I brought her a supply for when I visit."

"I never realized that you and Sylvia were so close."

"For many years," Grandma said, "even before you were born."

"Tell me." Tab settled back to listen. Her grandma's stories were always interesting and often had some kind of message. She considered it her duty to educate Tab, not only in the ways of the tribe but in the ways of life.

"When they were young mothers, Sylvia and your mom used to spend much time together. They worked on projects together, beading and knitting. My beautiful Emma was as dark and intense as the moon while Sylvia was blonde and bright. They both liked artful things. When Sylvia came into Billings to see *The Nutcracker* ballet, she stayed at your house."

Tab vaguely remembered going to the ballet when she was a little girl. Dancing wasn't her thing, but she loved getting all dressed up for the big performance.

"When Emma died," Grandma continued, "Sylvia was a comfort to me. And I returned the solace when she lost her husband. Why do you think I allowed you to spend that summer babysitting Misty instead of staying at my house?"

"To help Sylvia?"

"And to teach you a lesson. You never had brothers or sisters. Being with Misty showed you how to take care of another person who needed your help."

Since Tab ended up in a helping profession, she figured that the lesson had been well learned. "It might have been a turning point for me."

"Misty still needs our help," her grandma said.

"I want to stay here at the ranch until I know she's safe."

Tab understood the sentiment, but staying here wasn't practical. "They might never catch the murderer."

"They will," her grandma said in a tone of certainty that ended all discussion.

"What about Shua?"

"I already called the neighbors. Sam Tall Grass will take care of the horse and tend to the house. He's done it before."

Tab couldn't object on the basis of her business. All she needed was her cell phone to stay in contact with her clients, and she usually went to them instead of the other way around. The real problem with staying at the ranch was Aiden.

After last night's kiss, she couldn't pretend that he meant nothing to her. But she didn't want to rush into a relationship that was very likely to blow up in her face. "I'm not sure if we should stay."

Aiden came around the corner of the barn. Striding toward the house, he waved. Even at this distance, she could tell that he was grinning, and she couldn't help smiling back.

"A piece of advice," her grandma said.

"Yes?"

"Follow your heart."

Thanks, Yoda. But her heart wasn't crystal clear. She wanted to take a chance with him, but she was afraid. An old-fashioned cowboy who didn't want her involved in his investigating wouldn't be happy with a woman who thought for herself, took care of herself and made her own decisions.

The closer he got, the faster her heart beat. She moved to the edge of the porch. The soles of her feet were itching to run, either to dive into his arms or to charge past him and keep on going. Reaching up, she grasped the porch railing, anchoring herself. She'd stay. Just for today, she would stay.

Chapter Nine

"Good morning, Aiden."

Gazing down at him from the porch, Tab combined her memories with the current version of Aiden Gabriel and decided that, in the past, he might have been a little too pretty. Maturity suited him. He was one of those men who would get more chiseled and sexy as he aged, the lucky duck.

"Same to you." After a wink at her, he touched the brim of his hat and nodded to her grandmother. "Good morning, Maria Spotted Bear."

"I had a good sleep," Grandma announced.

"I always like to have you visit. When you're here, my mom opens up like a sunflower."

"I'm glad." She treated Aiden to one of her Buddha smiles. "Tab and I will stay here until I'm sure that Misty is safe."

Tab sucked in her cheeks to keep her embarrassment from showing. Who plopped themselves down on somebody else's porch and announced that they were moving in? Apparently, her grandma did. "That's a huge imposition. We really can't—"

"Your family is always welcome at the Gabriel ranch."

"Are you sure?"

"A hundred percent."

If she hadn't known the real history of Grandma and the Gabriel family, she would have been perplexed by Aiden's invitation. She was glad Grandma had told her about the deep, close relationship between her and Sylvia. Tragedies had brought them together. Friendship sealed their connection. The next logical step, she supposed, was the matchmaking.

With a glance at Aiden, she wondered about his remembrances of her mother. He'd been a teenager when she passed away, old enough to form an opinion. He might be able to reveal a different aspect of the past.

"Go now." Her grandma shooed them away. "You two young people should walk in the sunlight of a new day."

"Yes, ma'am." Aiden took Tab's hand and led her down the porch steps. As he escorted her along the sidewalk that led away from the front door, he asked, "Do you know what she means? Walking in the new sunlight?"

"It sounds cryptic and wise, doesn't it? Like something that might be said at a Sun Dance ritual. I'm pretty sure it doesn't mean anything more than Grandma wants to sit alone on the porch and relax."

"Have you ever seen a Sun Dance?"

"Once." The ceremony was no longer practiced on a regular basis. Few outsiders were invited to attend.

"I've heard it can be brutal."

His comment touched a nerve. "Don't you mean savage? As in those savages on the rez are doing their weird dances?"

"I didn't mean that at all."

"What have you heard?"

"Young men in the tribe are pierced at the breastbone and attached by a leather thong to a tall pole. Sometimes, they get hoisted off their feet. It's a rite of manhood."

With his thumbs hitched in his pockets and his dusty boots shuffling in a casual saunter, Aiden was every inch the cowboy. She couldn't expect him to understand the ways of her people. It was her heritage, and she barely understood. Hoping to dismiss the topic, she said, "Great weather, huh?"

"What does the Sun Dance mean to you?"

A fair question. Maybe he was sincerely interested, but years of prejudice had taught her to keep her guard up. She didn't want him to think of her as an exotic Crow princess, which she definitely was not. Her inclination was to shut down, but if she ever expected to have a *real* connection with the *real* Aiden, the flesh-and-blood man who walked beside her, she needed to open up.

"The Sun Dance isn't about macho or magic," she said. "The suffering of the young men is a form of prayer, like a sweat lodge or a vision quest. Their silent endurance brings blessings to their families. And, I assure you, their lives are never in danger. In the day-long ritual, we give thanks to the earth and ask for wisdom. Even as a kid, I was moved by the powerful sense of community."

"I appreciate the explanation."

"And it's not more brutal than rodeo bull riding."

At the end of the sidewalk, he leaned against a split-rail fence and turned his face up to catch the light. "Growing up, it must have been strange for you, moving back and forth between Billings and the rez. Did you feel like you belonged in the tribal community?"

"I could never choose between my home with my dad and my mother's people. I'm not totally one or the other." She took a sip from the coffee mug she'd carried with her. "When I was a kid on the rez, I got teased for my blue eyes. In Billings, people gave me a hard time about being Crow. Now, I enjoy having a foot in each world."

"Could be an asset in your midwife work."

"Exactly," she said. "Right now, I have only six

clients, and they're evenly divided between the rez and the people of Henley."

"You can make that seven clients," he said. "Misty wants you to deliver her baby."

"Did you talk to her last night?"

He nodded. "And you were right about her holding back something from the sheriff. The truth is that Misty didn't go to that party, but Clinton did. Misty sent him with the express purpose of getting the wristwatch back from Ellen Jessop."

Sending Clinton to the party didn't seem unreasonable, but she feared there was more to the story. "I'm guessing that Clinton argued with Ellen."

"Right," he said. "With Ellen ending up murdered, it looks bad for Clinton. I sure as hell don't want to think he had anything to do with her death, but he seems to be on the spot when people get killed. First, Ellen. Then, David."

"David?"

"Clinton is the most likely person to have picked up Misty's rifle and killed David."

"But he didn't," she said. "When I rode over the hill, Clinton was unconscious, sprawled in the back of the Jeep. I saw him. I'm his alibi."

"Was there enough time between when you heard the shots and when you rode over the hill for him to climb into the back of the Jeep?"

"Five or six minutes," she said quickly. Misty's story about the disappearing shooter made her very conscious of the time lapse. "Why would Clinton pretend to be unconscious?"

"You said it yourself. The concussion gave him an alibi."

After taking another sip, she stared down into her mug and swirled the remains of her coffee. Aiden had drawn a fairly logical conclusion, except for one thing. If Clinton had fired the shots that killed David Welling, Misty would have seen what happened. "Do you think Misty is lying to protect him?"

"If she is, she's not going to admit it. No matter how many times I ask, she keeps sticking to her story about the mysterious gunman."

"Maybe we should talk to Clinton," she suggested. "Not that I expect him to confess."

"Not at all." Aiden's hostility toward his sister's boyfriend showed in his body language. His eyebrows tensed in a scowl, and he folded his arms across his lean torso.

"He can't be that bad," she said. "Misty loves him."

"She also loves three-legged dogs, skunks and anybody with a sad story. My sister is a lousy judge of character."

"Still," she said, "it wouldn't hurt to talk to Clinton."

"He's not likely to open up to me. But you might get him to answer a couple of questions." He warmed to the idea. "You could start by asking him about the party and what happened when he tried to get the watch. Then, you'd ease the conversation around to what really happened when David Welling was killed."

"I could do that." She liked the direction Aiden was headed. Casually, she leaned against the fence beside him. "It almost sounds like you're asking me to help."

"Does it now?"

"You bet it does. It's almost like we're investigating. Both of us. Together." She covered her smug grin by draining the last of her coffee. "I seem to recall something you said about not wanting my help because it was too... What was it you said? It was too dangerous for a delicate flower like me."

"I'm real damn sure I never called you a flower."

"I added that part," she said. "You know what you said."

He shoved away from the fence and stood tall before her. "If you're done with your I-told-you-so, I'd like to put things into motion. Clinton is in the horse barn."

"And you want me to talk to him." She looked up through her eyelashes. "You want me to help you investigate."

"I reckon I do."

"Consider it done." She handed him her coffee mug. "I'll see you back at the house."

LOCATING CLINTON wasn't difficult. All Tab had to do was follow the smell. As the lowest employee on the totem pole, he had the most boring assignment—mucking out the stalls in the horse barn. He was more than happy to abandon his shaving fork and follow her outside to the corral where the horses were at the troughs.

Tab used the most obvious excuse to get their conversation started. "I wanted to see how you were doing after your head injury. Looks like somebody changed the dressing."

"My mom," he said as he pulled off his rubber gloves and flexed his fingers. "Just like you, she wanted me to go to the doctor."

"But you didn't go."

"I'm fine." When she reached toward the bandages, he jerked his head back and settled his baseball cap more firmly on the top of his head. "Really, I'm okay."

"How did you sleep?"

"Good."

She tugged his arm and pulled him closer to the corral gate. "Step over here into the sunlight and let me look at your eyes. I want to see if your pupils are dilated."

Reluctantly, he stared at her. Up close and quiet, he was more appealing than when he was strutting around, trying to impress Misty. Not a bad-looking kid, but he was young, so very young to be taking on the responsibilities of fatherhood.

"You need to be careful with a concussion," she said. "Have you noticed double vision or dizziness?"

He shook his head.

"Ringing in your ears? Persistent headache? Are you having any trouble focusing or remembering?"

"No, no and no."

"If any of those things crop up, I advise you to see a doctor. You're fortunate not to have any serious problem, at least not a physical problem." She studied him with a calm, measured stare. "In other ways, you're very unlucky."

"What's that supposed to mean?"

"You've got a talent for being in the wrong place at the wrong time." She remembered Aiden's accusation. *First, Ellen. Then, David.* "What happened when you went to the party and talked to Ellen Jessop?"

"Misty wanted me to get her gold watch. She said she'd pay Ellen to get it back, but I knew that wouldn't work. Ellen's family might have lost all their money, but she's still got her pride."

"How well did you know Ellen?"

"We had a couple of dates. She was pretty and blonde, tall with long legs. But, damn, she had a temper. She'd get so angry that I thought she'd bite my head off. And jealous."

And now she was dead, horribly murdered. He didn't seem too concerned about her death. "Did you like her?"

He eyed her suspiciously. "I've got nothing else to say."

As a midwife, Tab was accustomed to working with obstinate young people who were confused and scared. When it was time for the baby to be born, the fathers were usually more freaked out than the mothers. She'd learned how to talk them down.

"I want to help you, Clinton. Believe me when I say that I know what you're going through. You're trying to take care of Misty, but there's nobody for you to lean on."

His mouth pinched in a tight knot. "Especially not Aiden."

"I understand." She knew better than to get sidetracked by a discussion of Aiden. "Here's the deal, Clinton. Misty wants me to be her midwife, and that means you need to trust me. We have to work together. Okay?"

"I guess."

"I want the whole story about what's been going on with you and Misty and these terrible crimes," she said. "You can start by telling me about what happened between you and Ellen."

"She acted like she owned every minute of my time. We only went out two times and I never slept with her, but she got mad when I talked to other girls."

"Did she blame Misty for your breakup?"

"That's right." He nodded. "Misty and me didn't get together until three or four months after I ended things with Ellen, but somehow she thought Misty stole me away from her."

Once his barriers were down, Clinton had a lot to say. He couldn't stop his mouth from running as he described typical teenage incidents of two girls fighting over one guy. Though his story was mostly a boost for his own ego, he seemed truly perplexed about these two women.

Though he had a motive for disliking Ellen, the love triangle didn't seem like enough for murder. In an attempt to rein him in, she said, "What about the party?"

"I tried to talk nice to her, but she got louder and louder. She said mean things about Misty, and it made me so mad that I made a grab for the watch. Ellen drew back her hand, slapped me hard and threw her beer in my face."

"Did you threaten her?"

"No, ma'am. My mom and dad taught me never to hit a woman. I turned around and walked away. Last time I saw her. Now, she's dead." His mouth got tight again. "Was it the serial killer?"

Though the sheriff had avoided labeling the murders as a serial killing, Tab knew the gossip train would race toward the most sensational theory. One dead girl was an event. Two pointed to a serial killer. "I don't know."

"That's what people in town are saying."

"Those folks aren't always right. Did you hear about Woody and Chuck?"

"Misty called me and told me what they did last night. Damn, it makes me mad. How could they think that Misty was a murderer?"

"Some people think you're the one who shot David Welling." Offering him an easy out, she continued, "In self-defense."

"Even if I'd been awake and I saw him threaten Misty, I wouldn't need a gun to take him." He raised both fists. "I'd use these."

"You didn't like David."

"He was always sniffing around, acting like Misty was his secret lover. Well, she wasn't. She's my girl."

His anger sounded like the ravings of a seventeen-year-old, but Tab sensed something deeper and perhaps more sinister. "What are you hiding, Clinton?"

"Nothing."

"You can trust me," she encouraged him. "Is it something about David?"

"Some things are private." He glared. "Everybody thinks I'm stupid, but all of you smart people, including Sheriff Fielding, keep looking in the wrong direction for the killer."

"Fine," she said. "Tell me the right direction."

"Misty told you the God's honest truth. Somebody used her gun to shoot David, and then they ran off. All you've got to do is find their car."

"If there was a mystery shooter..."

"That's the only way it could have happened." He paced away from her and came back again. "We were smack dab in the middle of nowhere. How did David get there? He must have had some kind of transportation."

"Of course."

"Where did it go? What happened to David's car?" He poked a finger at her to make his point. "I'll tell you what happened, the only thing that could have happened. The mystery shooter used David's car to make his getaway."

"Find the car, and we find the killer."

His logic had a simple elegance that didn't fit with his scruffy appearance. David needed transportation to get to the riverbed where he confronted Misty, but his car was gone. Therefore, somebody drove it away. If that were true, Misty's story about the disappearing killer had some credence.

There was more to him than met the eye. For the first time, Tab thought he might just be worthy of Misty.

Chapter Ten

Aiden still didn't like the idea of Tab being involved in investigating, but he was impressed with how much information she'd gotten from Clinton. When she asked if she could hitch a ride into Henley with him, he hadn't refused. His plan was to talk to Bert Welling at the gas station and find out what kind of vehicle David had been driving. He didn't expect his conversation with David's uncle to be easy, especially since half the town believed that Misty was the killer. But Aiden had known Bert for years and had given him a lot of business. That ought to count for something.

Driving down the road they'd flown over last night, he noticed that Woody's truck was still parked on the shoulder. "I wonder if those two boys are still in jail."

"I hope the sheriff doesn't let them off easy," Tab said. "They need to know that pranks using guns won't be tolerated."

"A hard lesson. Guns are part of life around here."

"And Montana gun laws are practically nonexistent," she said. "That makes me wonder why Misty's mystery shooter wasn't armed. Why did he need to use Misty's rifle."

"It was an opportunity. He saw the gun and figured he could frame my sister." Once Aiden accepted Misty's story, it made all kinds of sense. "The mystery shooter and David must have come there together, probably following Misty."

"Because David had a crush," she said.

"I hope that's all it was." He didn't like to think about Misty being targeted for a darker reason. "After the murder, the shooter used the vehicle for his getaway."

"Find the car, and we find the killer," she said.

"It's not that simple," he said. "Like the mystery shooter, this vehicle is invisible…and silent. Neither you nor Misty heard an engine starting up."

"The rush of the river could have covered the engine noise."

"When I flew over, I didn't see a vehicle."

"He made a quick escape," she said. "There had to be a car for David to get to the site, and it was pretty clever of Clinton to focus on that. It wouldn't hurt for you to tell him he was helpful. Whether you like it or not, he's going to be a permanent part of your family."

"It'll take more than a single flash of intelligence for me to change my mind about him."

"You have an opportunity to mend fences. Don't build a wall instead." Unexpectedly, she chuckled. "I can't believe I said that. I'm starting to sound like Grandma Yoda."

Her laughter drew him closer. It had been a while since he'd had a pretty woman riding in the passenger seat of his truck. When he was still in his long-distance relationship, he hadn't gone out with anyone else, and it wasn't only because he was being faithful. None of the local women interested him. Not until Tab arrived.

Today, she wore her hair pulled back in a low ponytail fastened with an orange-and-blue beaded barrette. She looked fresh and young. The unbraided length of her blue-black hair shimmered in the sunlight, and he longed to tangle his fingers in the silky strands.

"When we get to town," she said, "you can drop me off at the café on the corner of Main and Grant. That's where I'm meeting with my client."

"At the café?"

"She's a waitress, nine months pregnant. She called this morning and said the baby wasn't kicking as much, maybe only once or twice an hour. Sometimes, that's a sign that the mom is about to go into labor."

Aiden had participated in the delivery of cows,

horses and other livestock, but it was hard for him to imagine a human woman giving birth. "I know who you're talking about. Her name is Connie, right? If she thinks she's going to have the baby, why did she go to work?"

"I told her to stay home, but she wanted to pick up the morning shift. She said her tips have been phenomenal since she started showing."

He nodded. "I've been slipping an extra couple of bucks under the plate when she's my waitress. And I've been feeling like I ought to help her carry something."

"Anyway, this is just a quick checkup. I'll pop in and say hi. Then I'll catch up with you at the gas station."

Aiden hesitated before replying. He wanted to draw the line about how involved she should be. Though he had no particular reason to suspect Bert, he didn't want Tab associated with his investigating. "I'd rather have you wait for me at the café."

"Why?"

"I'll meet you there for coffee. I've got a taste for one of their sweet rolls."

"I don't believe that. You just had breakfast," she said. "Why are you trying to keep me away from the gas station?"

"For your own safety." He could have made up a lie, but he knew she'd see through him. "I don't want any focus on you. We could be dealing with a serial killer, somebody who brutalizes and rapes his victims."

"Are you talking about Bert Welling? The man who runs the tidiest gas station in the state?"

"I don't know where the danger is coming from. That's the problem."

"Is it?" Her tone was frosty. "It seems to me that all you're doing is asking questions, which is exactly what I did with Clinton. I can help. That's why Grandma wants us to stay at your house. To help. To find the real killer so Misty won't be accused."

They drove past the scattered houses at the outskirts of town. The bad economy had taken a toll in this area. Some of these homes were boarded up and abandoned. Families were leaving Henley and moving to Billings where they'd have a better chance of finding steady work. Aiden feared that the small-town way of life he'd always cherished was coming to an end.

His world was changing before his eyes. He shouldn't be looking for a serial killer. Those kinds of crimes belonged in the big city, not in his sleepy little town. It used to be that Gabriel ranch commanded so much respect that nobody would dare to drive by and shoot off their guns, much less to accuse Misty of murder. *Changes.* Everything was turning upside down, and the worst part was how these changes struck close to home. His baby sister was about to become a single mother. His church-going mom seemed content to sleep with Blake and not marry him.

His idea of shielding Tab from the dangers of an investigation might be part of a bygone era when the menfolk did the protecting and the womenfolk stayed home and baked pies. Tab sure as hell didn't fit that mold. If she had, he probably wouldn't have found her so appealing.

"Fine," he said. "Meet me at the gas station when you're done."

"I intend to." The chill in her voice turned crisp and professional. "And I'm coming along this afternoon when you take off in the chopper."

That suited him just fine. In the chopper with him, she'd be safe. "Glad to have you along."

"Good, because I need to stop by Grandma's house and pick up some clothes and basic supplies. Also, I want to bring Shua over here to the ranch. I know the neighbors are taking care of her, but I worry she's not getting enough exercise."

He suppressed an urge to warn her about riding all across the countryside by herself. Yesterday, he'd sent her off without being worried. But that was before they'd found Ellen, the second victim of the serial killer.

They drove down Main Street, a wide two-lane road with angled parking on both sides. Like the outlying area, the shops along the sidewalk showed signs of deterioration although most of the storefronts were occupied. At the far end of the street, two churches faced each other. Half a mile beyond was Henley High, home of the Bobcats.

Aiden drove past the gas station with a green neon open sign in the front window. Apparently, Bert Welling wasn't taking off any time to mourn his murdered nephew. Two blocks away at the café, he dropped Tab off.

She waved. "See you in a few."

Circling back, he drove up to the gas pump where the price for regular was a whole lot higher than he liked to pay. Aiden climbed down from the cab as Bert emerged from the office. Dressed in the gray jumpsuit with his name stitched over the breast pocket, Bert looked much too neat and tidy to be a car mechanic, but that was his way.

Ever since he took over the gas station, more than a dozen years ago, he'd adhered to a standard of cleanliness more typical of a tea parlor than a garage. From the spotless windows to the array of tools neatly hung on pegs, Bert's station showed a compulsive attention to order and detail.

Aiden took off his hat and extended his hand. "I'm sorry for your loss."

Bert acknowledged his words with a nod. His clean-shaven face was without expression. Not a single strand of his thinning black hair dared to slip out of place. "Fill 'er up?"

"Yes, sir. And I'm due for an oil change, if you've got the time."

"Drive 'er into the first bay."

Aiden followed Bert's instruction, figuring that while the two of them were inside the garage together, he might be more prone to conversation. Or maybe not. Bert was never the talkative sort.

As Bert moved efficiently through his routine for getting the truck up on the lift, Aiden decided to forego subtlety. "There's been talk that my sister was somehow responsible for David's death. I want you to know it's not true."

"I don't blame Misty," Bert said. "David always spoke highly of her. She was a cut above most of the girls he dated."

"I expect you've heard about Chuck and Woody."

"They're not bad kids. They've worked for me. It takes a lot of effort to keep this place in good repair."

Aiden imagined the teenagers scrubbing the concrete floor in the auto bays with a toothbrush to meet Bert's standards. The image didn't fit into the sheriff's idea of a gang. "You hire a lot of local kids. That's a damn good thing. They need the jobs."

"I'm not a do-gooder," he said as he pulled on a pair of gloves. "I hire people to do a job."

"Have you met this new guy they call Aspen Jim?"

"David brought him. I didn't bother getting to know him. A handsome devil like Jim won't stick around Henley too long. He's a skier. He'll be heading for snow country."

The sheriff had suggested that Aspen Jim was a ringleader. "He's a little older than the high school boys you usually hire."

"Never noticed."

Aspen Jim was an anomaly. A good-looking, mature ski bum didn't fit into the fabric of Henley. This wasn't a glamorous place. The skiing industry in Montana was nothing compared to Jackson Hole in Wyoming or Park City in Utah or any of the Colorado resorts. "Why would a guy like that want to live here? A girlfriend?"

"Don't know. Don't care."

"Yoo-hoo." Tab's voice echoed against the concrete walls of the garage.

"Back here," Bert called out.

She marched up to him and took both his gloved hands in hers. Her blue eyes welled with sympathy. "I'm so sorry about David, Mr. Welling. Can I drop by later with one of Grandma's sweet potato pies?"

Much to Aiden's surprise, Bert cracked a smile. "I'd never say no to one of Maria Spotted Bear's pies."

"Will you be having the funeral here?"

"That's his dad's problem. He lives in Billings." Bert dropped her hands. His thin face became a blank. "My brother, David's dad, did a bad job in raising the boy after his mom left. The least he can do is to arrange for a proper burial."

Tab tilted her head. Her lovely face glowed with kindness, and Aiden knew it wasn't an act. She was able to sincerely look past Bert's natural hostility and see the sadness within. More important, Bert responded to her.

"You spent a lot of time with David," she said. "Showed him the right way to do things."

"But he still ended up dead. David had a weak character, just like his dad. My brother is nothing but a self-pitying, sloppy alcoholic." His gaze lifted, and he frowned as though he'd spotted a spider's web in the corner of the ceiling. "At least David stayed off the booze."

"I'm sure you'll miss him."

"He wasn't good at following instructions. Couldn't remember to clean up after himself. His van was filthy."

Aiden pounced on the possible lead. "What kind of van?"

"Why do you care?"

"I might be in the market to buy a van for Misty to use after she has the baby."

"Go ahead and take a look. The thing looks like crud, but it runs just fine." Bert shrugged. "It's parked in back of the garage. I told David that until he got a paint job, he couldn't park at the house."

As Aiden walked to the front of the garage, Tab patted the sleeve of Bert's clean jumpsuit. "If you need anything, don't hesitate to call. Grandma and I are staying at the Gabriel Ranch."

"I didn't know you were all that close."

"Family friends," Tab said.

"Somebody told me you were there when David got shot. But you didn't see who did it."

"I was too late," she said, "but don't you worry. The sheriff is investigating. He'll find the killer."

She joined him. Together, they circled the whitewashed side of the garage. The back side where the trash cans were kept was slightly less tidy than the front. A beat-up van with a dinged front fender was parked with the nose facing to a light pole.

"I have a change of plans," Tab said. "My client's water broke about a half hour ago, and her husband just got to the café to pick her up. I think she's ready to go into labor, so I need to go back to the ranch, get my stuff and meet her at her house."

He couldn't have been more pleased. Tab was off the case. "A real shame," he drawled, "you won't be able to do any more investigating today."

"Babies come first."

"Do you need to hurry? Is this an emergency?"

"Not really," she said. "It's a first baby. I'd expect her to be in labor for hours."

Turning back to the van, he squatted to check out the tires and the tire wells. Dried weeds were stuck in the treads and wedged behind the mud flaps. "This van was driven off the road. It might be the vehicle David used yesterday."

"And the shooter drove it back," she said. "He might have left his fingerprints on the car keys."

"Even if he did, the prints can be explained if it's one of David's friends."

"How can we find out who he was with yester day?"

"We can't go around asking those kinds of questions." Aiden rose to his feet. "I'll suggest to the sheriff that he might want to talk to David's buddies about their whereabouts yesterday. Woody and Chuck are already in custody. Maybe they'll say something useful, instead of being twin jackasses."

She dragged her fingertip through the dust on the back window. "Apparently, David didn't inherit his uncle's obsessive neatness."

He circled around to the front of the van. There was a bike rack mounted on the hood. Two mountain bikes with heavy-duty tires were locked in place. If Misty's mystery shooter hopped onto a bike and rode through the foliage at the river bank, they wouldn't have heard a car engine starting. Hiding a bike would have been far easier than ditching a car or a van.

"Take a look at this," he called to her. "These are really nice bikes. Expensive."

Another voice intruded, "And I've got first dibs."

The man who sauntered toward them had a tanned complexion and sun-streaked hair that flopped casually over his forehead. He wore wrap-around sunglasses and a lightweight parka with the hood zipped into the collar. His super-whitened smile flashed as he came even with Tab. This had to be Aspen Jim.

Chapter Eleven

Tab looked at dual reflections of herself in a pair of gleaming sunglasses. The man wearing them took her hand and raised it to his lips. "They call me Aspen Jim."

"I'm Tab Willows." When meeting new people, she tried to keep an open mind, but this guy creeped her out. He reminded her of a lounge lizard without the lounge.

He whipped off his sunglasses, revealing bloodshot brown eyes. "Why haven't I met you before?"

"Just lucky, I guess." She snatched her hand from his grasp. "This is Aiden Gabriel."

"I know who you are. Misty's brother." Aspen Jim replaced his sunglasses on the narrow bridge of his nose. "I'm pleased to meet you, Aiden. How's your sister doing?"

"As well as can be expected," Aiden said, "after watching David die in her arms."

"He liked her a lot, even after she ballooned up."

"That's a nasty thing to say." Tab hated men

who made snide comments about pregnant women. "Women are at their most beautiful when they're carrying new life. Artists have always celebrated the pregnant form as a symbol of fertility."

"Not me," Aspen Jim said. "I like my ladies slim and sexy. Kind of like you, darling."

"Have you ever made love to a pregnant woman?"

"No way."

"Then you're missing something spectacular. Several men have told me that it's the most exciting sex they ever had."

"Why would they tell you?"

"I'm a midwife." She looked at her wristwatch. "And I need to get going."

"Hold on a sec." Aiden stepped forward. She noticed that his lips barely moved when he spoke, and she suspected he was gritting his teeth to keep from snarling. "Mind if I ask you a couple of questions, Aspen Jim?"

"No prob." Blinded by arrogance, Aspen Jim didn't realize that he ought to be nervous about Aiden's questions. "I'm glad for the chance to talk to you."

"First, tell me about these bikes."

"They're top of the line." Aspen Jim turned away from her and went to the bikes and lovingly caressed the handlebars. "Titanium frame, dual suspension and hydraulic disc brakes, these bikes have it all."

"Did they both belong to David?"

"Yeah, and he never really appreciated these super-fine machines, the little dipstick." He winced. "Sorry, I didn't mean to say that. 'Dipstick' was kind of a nickname."

Tab didn't believe that for a minute. Aspen Jim was the kind of guy who used his friends and badmouthed them behind their backs. She was beginning to feel sorry for David Welling with his alcoholic father, his cold-as-ice uncle and a friend like Aspen Jim.

"The bikes must have been expensive," Aiden said.

"David got them in trade for doing mechanical work on a Ferrari for some rich dude in Billings. We used to take them out and ride all over. It's important for me to stay in good condition for skiing."

"Were you out riding yesterday?"

"The weather's been great—didn't want to miss it." Aspen Jim hesitated, perhaps realizing that he'd stepped into what might be a stinky alibi situation. "It was early, like ten in the morning."

Smoothly, Aiden asked, "Where did you go? There's a lot of nice, wide open land on the rez."

"I don't know the boundaries. We might have gone there."

"Did anybody see you leaving town or coming back?"

Aspen Jim lowered his chin, and his sun-bleached

bangs flopped over the frames of his sunglasses. When he looked up, his glistening smile had vanished. "I wasn't with David when he got killed, if that's what you're trying to figure out."

"Tell me what happened."

Tab was duly impressed with Aiden's questioning. Though he didn't have the credentials to demand information, he showed enough authority in his voice and manner that Aspen Jim was beginning to sweat.

"Me and David took the van with the bikes out in the morning after we had pancakes at the café with Woody and Chuck. We rode the bikes for a while, and then headed back to town. David was kind of mopey."

"Why?" Aiden asked.

"He couldn't decide whether he should stay here in Henley, or go back to Billings and live with his dad. Then he spotted Misty in Clinton's Jeep, and he said it was a sign. He was going to talk to her. If she said he should stay, he would."

"But he didn't have that kind of relationship with my sister. They didn't chat, didn't text each other."

"Only in David's head," Aspen Jim said. "He was always planning to talk to Misty. She was his dream girl."

"So he followed the Jeep," Aiden said.

"That was his plan. I didn't stick around. I took one of the bikes and rode the rest of the way home."

"Did you hook up with Woody and Chuck again?"

Aspen Jim shook his head. "It was my day off. I took a long shower, watched some TV, played a couple of computer games. Then I brought the bike back here and left it with Bert."

"What time was that?"

"Maybe three o'clock, I don't remember. Bert probably can tell you down to the minute. He's precise."

Tab was disappointed to hear that he had an alibi. If Aspen Jim was here at the gas station, he couldn't have committed the crime. Too bad.

"When you dropped off the bike," Aiden said, "was David's van here?"

"No, it wasn't. That's why I handed the bike over to Bert. I didn't hear what happened to David until around seven when I went to the Last Stand Tavern."

"You should have gone to the sheriff right away," Tab said. "Your information might have been useful to him."

"I don't much care for the law. I don't have anything to hide, but I don't want anybody getting into my business."

"But you're willing to talk to me."

"That's correct." He stuck out his chest. "I'm glad for this opportunity to meet you."

"Is that so?"

"I have a business opportunity you might be interested in. I'm looking for investors."

Disgusted, Tab rolled her eyes. Aspen Jim really was a piece of work. His friend hadn't been dead for twenty-four hours, and he was figuring out how to cash in. Brusquely, she said, "We don't have time for this."

"Here's my idea," Aspen Jim said. "I want to provide river rafting expeditions on the Little Big Horn. When the tourists show up for the reenactment of Custer's Last Stand, this gives them something else to do."

"There's white-water rafting on the Yellowstone," Aiden said, "because that river actually has rapids. The Little Big Horn rolls along, slow and lazy."

"So it's perfect for families. Hey, here's a thought. We could hire locals to stand on the banks and act out scenes from the Old West."

Tab groaned.

Aiden asked, "How much do you know about rafting?"

He flashed the super-white smile. "I worked as a guide with a rafting crew on the Arkansas River near Aspen. Think about it, Aiden. With your cash and my expertise, we could have the business up and running by next summer."

Tab had heard enough. She clamped on to Aiden's arm. "We really have to go. Now."

They left Aspen Jim standing by the van, paid for the oil change and climbed into the truck. As soon as they were under way, she let loose. "Do you believe that guy? I think he was lurking around, waiting to pounce the minute he saw you. Rafting on the Little Big Horn? Acting out scenes on the banks? Oh, please, that's the dumbest thing I've ever heard."

"But now we know why a flashy guy like him is hanging around in Henley."

"He wants to con somebody into being his partner. What a jerk! I'll bet he's already screwed up his big money contacts in the ski areas."

"He worked as a guide for a white-water rafting company. That means he knows about nautical knots."

She wasn't sure where Aiden was going with this. "So?"

"When I was talking to the sheriff…" His voice trailed off. "I shouldn't tell you about this, Tab. But you're the only one I can talk to, and I respect your opinions."

Now they were making headway. He wasn't shutting her out of his investigation anymore. "What's important about the knots?"

"Both of the women who were killed were bound with bowlines and figure eights. Nautical knots."

She hadn't expected this twist. "Do you think Aspen Jim is the serial killer?"

"Knowing about knots isn't enough to accuse him," Aiden said. "But he did know Ellen Jessop. They worked together at the feed store."

Staring through the windshield at the dried prairie grasses on rolling hills, she recalibrated her thinking to include the serial murders. Their trip into town to see Bert had been focused on David's death, but they couldn't ignore the possible link. Misty was clearly connected to both since she had argued with Ellen and had witnessed David's murder.

"Next time you talk to the sheriff, you definitely need to mention Aspen Jim as a suspect."

"Sheriff Fielding is already looking at Aspen Jim." He shrugged. "I don't think he seems like the serial killer type. He wouldn't have a problem getting dates. A lot of women might like that sun-bleached hair."

"Not me," she said. "Aspen Jim is a misogynist, the kind of guy who hates women. Didn't you hear what he said about pregnant ladies?"

"I sure as hell heard what you said." He glanced at her and grinned. "Pregnant sex is spectacular?"

"So I've heard." At the time she'd spoken, she'd been trying to make a point that an idiot like Aspen Jack would understand. She hadn't considered how embarrassing her statement would sound. "I'm not an expert."

"You're a surprising lady, Tab. I'm learning that

I don't know much about your world and the work you do."

When guys asked about her work, she usually retreated into her shell. They weren't really interested, just being polite. But Aiden was different, and she wanted him to understand her. "How much do you want to know?"

"Everything," he said.

"Starting with the sperm and the egg?"

"Especially about that part."

When it came to flirting, her skills were nonexistent. She preferred saying exactly what she meant, but it was fun to play with Aiden. She keyed her voice to a low, sexy level and said, "I have a feeling that you already know a little something about the fertilization process."

"I like it when you talk dirty."

His jaw twitched as he struggled to keep from laughing out loud. When she punched his arm, he chuckled, and she joined in. A sense of humor wasn't something she associated with the super-responsible Aiden, but here they were...joking around with each other.

It would have been nice to extend this time together. She almost wished she didn't have to go to work, but there was no way to reschedule her client's labor. The truck was already approaching the crossroads that led to Gabriel Ranch, and she'd have to jump into her van and leave immediately.

"We don't have much time," he said. "I wanted to get your impressions of Aspen Jim's account of what happened yesterday."

"It sounded pretty straightforward. And he's got a solid alibi with Bert. The real question is who drove David's van back to the gas station?"

"Chuck and Woody might have known where they were headed. It could have been one of them."

"Could be." Neither Chuck nor Woody seemed dangerous to her. Last night when they were forced to stop the truck, they both surrendered without hesitation. "Why would one of David's friends shoot him?"

"We don't know enough about David to come up with a motive."

Aiden took off his hat and raked his fingers through his hair. When he gazed toward her, his eyes gleamed. For a moment, she forgot about investigating and murders and the baby she was about to deliver. His nearness consumed her, and she couldn't think of anything else.

Until now, she'd done a pretty decent job of acting like an adult instead of a love-struck teenager. But there were these moments when she was with him that she had to pinch herself to make sure she wasn't dreaming.

"What were we talking about?" she asked.

"Motives."

"I've got nothing."

He slapped his hat back onto his head and turned his attention to the road. "What if David was killed because he knew too much? He might have figured out the identity of the serial killer and was threatening to tell the sheriff."

She nodded. "That doesn't tell us who the killer is."

"But it limits the field."

For the first time, she acknowledged to herself that there might be danger. If David knew the killer, so did Misty. And it was likely that Tab had met him. She didn't know his identity, but he knew hers.

Chapter Twelve

The birthing had gone well. A little before eight o'clock, Tab parked her van outside the Gabriel Ranch, hopped out and strode toward the house. When she saw Aiden occupying the rocking chair on the porch where her grandma had been sitting this morning, she couldn't help grinning. He'd been waiting for her. *Sweet.*

As she approached, he stood and sauntered down the stairs. The porch lights shone behind him, silhouetting his long, lean body, wide shoulders and cowboy hat. She had the sense that she was coming home to him, to her perfect man.

"You look happy," he said.

"I love my job. There's nothing as exciting as bringing new life into the world. When I hold the wiggly baby for the first time and hear the first cries, I feel privileged to be part of a miracle. Seven pounds and two ounces, the baby's name is Rosalie."

"Pretty name."

"Pretty little girl." She wanted to hug him and share the thrill but held herself back. The Gabriel Ranch wasn't really her home. Aiden didn't belong to her, and she didn't have the right to grab him whenever she had the urge. "You'll see. When Misty has her baby, you'll see what it feels like."

"I've been around babies before."

"Trust me. A newborn is different."

"Are you tired?"

"I should be after six hours of labor. Not that I did any of the heavy-duty exertion, but the process is a strain."

"How so?"

She tried to think of a metaphor that he'd understand. "You played football, didn't you?"

"Henley High," he said. "Go, Bobcats. And in college."

"Think of a football game, and think of me as the coach. I don't actually run down the field with the ball, but I call the plays and I strategize."

"I don't reckon you choose to punt too often."

"Very funny." The football comparison might have been a bad idea.

"Go on. Tell me what happens after the huddle."

"Mostly, it's about making the mom comfortable, giving her water or tea or sometimes a snack. Some women have pressure on their lower spine, and that means a lot of back rubs. Sometimes, I'll get the mom out of bed and walk around. The last phase of labor, which is called transition, can be intense. That's the dramatic part that you always see in movies."

"When the baby comes out, that's your touchdown."

"But I never spike the baby in the end zone."

"Because that would be a penalty," he said. "Well, Coach, I'm thinking you might need some rest."

"I won't be able to sleep." After a birthing, she was energized. "My endorphins are rushing. I feel good all over."

He reached toward her and placed his hand on her shoulder, setting off a whole different kind of pleasurable reaction. His touch soothed her and aroused her at the same time.

"Let's get you to bed," he said.

She really wanted to say yes, not to the sleeping part but to going to bed with him. Instead, she shook her head.

"I'd rather hop in the chopper and go to Grandma's house." She'd called earlier to let him know that she still needed to pick up a few things from home. "I won't ride Shua back tonight, but I'd really like to have a change of clothes, my own nightshirt and toothbrush."

"You're sure?"

She cocked her head to one side. "Could it be that you're the one who's too tired?"

"Not me. My day hasn't been action packed." He slid his hand down her arm and linked his hand with hers. "Let's go."

Holding hands, they walked together through the moonlight toward the barn. She rubbed her thumb across the calluses on his palm. Rough hands were an occupational hazard for cowboys who worked with horses and cattle in all kinds of weather. When he squeezed her fingers, electricity jolted up her arm and raced through her entire body. Were they really holding hands?

A pine-scented breeze cooled her cheeks and ruffled the strands of hair that had slipped out of her ponytail. With her free hand, she pushed her hair back. "I must look a mess."

"Not with that beautiful smile lighting up your face. You look great."

His words warmed her but didn't erase her self-consciousness. As her body heated up, she remembered that she hadn't used deodorant after her shower this morning. A change of clothing was definitely needed. Though she'd slipped into comfortable scrubs for the labor and birthing, the shirt she'd worn for the past two days was getting a little ripe.

"After a big game," he said, "I always liked to talk about the plays that worked and the slipups. Give me the rundown on what happened today with—what are their names? Connie and Carlos?"

"I will if you promise not to mention football again. Having a baby isn't really the Wide World of Sports."

"Promise." He ducked his head to look into her eyes. "But I would like to hear about it. If I'm going to understand what you do, you've got to give me some details."

"When I got to the house, Connie greeted me with a paintbrush in her hand. Apparently, the nursery needed another coat, and she wanted it done before the baby arrived."

"Is that typical?" he asked.

"Different women handle the stress and hormones in different ways. Connie obsessed on cleaning. Even though Carlos promised to take care of the painting, she refused to get into bed. On the internet, she'd read that just because her water broke it didn't mean she was in labor."

"Was she right?"

"Obviously not," Tab said. "I just delivered the baby. I encourage new moms to seek out prenatal information. The more they know, the less scared they are. The downside to that approach is that they think they're experts. Connie felt a little twinge and announced that it was a Braxton Hicks contraction, false labor."

"I'm beginning to feel sorry for Carlos."

"He's a really nice guy, but Connie was driving him crazy. When I finally convinced her to surrender the paintbrush and let me give her an exam, he whispered that I must be an angel sent from Heaven to keep his wife from killing him."

"I've heard that women get mean during labor."

"With good cause," she said. "Having a baby isn't easy."

"What did you do next?"

She decided to skip the clinical description of how she assessed Connie's dilation and effacement. Aiden's interest in her work probably didn't extend to all the gory details. "After I checked her out, I knew she was starting labor. Her pain started getting more intense, and we were off to the races. Six hours later, Rosalie came into the world."

"Giving birth is easier with cows," he said. "They give a couple of bellows and shoot the baby right out. If the calf is stuck, you just reach inside, grab and pull."

"You might not want to share that comparison with your sister."

They circled the barn, and the helicopter came into view. Last night when she'd been running hard, she hadn't really appreciated the beauty of the machine. With moonlight reflecting off the rotors and long tail, the chopper looked like a giant mechanical dragonfly.

He gave her hand another squeeze before releasing it and digging into his pocket. He took out a sheet of notebook paper that was covered with tight scribbling. Handing it to her, he said, "Your grandma made a list of things she needs."

Tab held the paper close so she could read it in the moonlight. "Half of this is kitchen equipment. Pots and skillets and spices. Why does she need this stuff?"

He opened the cockpit door. "Hop aboard. You know the drill."

She strapped herself into the copilot seat, put on her headphones and prepared for the incredible sensation of swooping into the night sky. Their ascent tonight wasn't as incredible as when she was a chopper virgin, but the thrill was undiminished. She didn't think she'd ever become jaded about flying.

As they soared over the rugged landscape and approached the lights of Henley, she asked, "Did you do any more investigating today?"

"I spent most of the day with the sheriff. He's leaning toward our theory of David being shot by an unknown companion who rode off on a mountain bike. But he still won't dismiss Misty as a suspect."

"What does he think of Aspen Jim?"

"It's a shame Aspen Jim has an alibi. Nobody trusts him except for his teenage buddies, including Woody and Chuck, who think he's a lot of fun. Remember how the Buffalo Man talked about loud parties in the deserted parts of the rez? According to Woody and Chuck, who were both feeling real bad after a night in jail, Aspen Jim provided the booze."

"At least, it wasn't drugs."

"As far as we know." He adjusted the steering to swoop toward the left. "The sheriff agreed with me. Aspen Jim has all the girlfriends he wants. He's a sleazy guy, but he doesn't fit the profile for a serial killer."

Though she respected the psychology that went into profiling, she didn't consider it proof. Serial killers came in all sizes and shapes; they didn't have to look like depraved, drooling monsters. The infamous Ted Bundy had been a handsome, educated, socially adept man who brutally murdered more than twenty women.

When she met Aspen Jim, she'd thought he was mean spirited. The way he looked at her made her skin crawl. His whitened teeth and sun-bleached hair didn't mean he was innocent.

"Anything else?" she asked. "How about the autopsies?"

"The coroner's office in Billings won't get around to a full autopsy for a couple more days, and they're going to start with Ellen Jessop. All the branches of law enforcement—state, local and tribal—are worried about the possibility of a serial killer. There's been talk of calling in the FBI."

She understood why the murder of David Welling wasn't as high priority, but the lack of investigation didn't relieve the stress on Misty. She really wished that she and Aiden could find evidence that would take his sister off the list of suspects. "If David's murder was somehow connected to the others, it would be more important. The sheriff seemed pretty sure that Misty's watch was some kind of evidence."

"Here's the thing," he said. "In a small town, everybody knows everybody else's business. There's just not much population, and it's hard to believe that there's more than one homicidal individual on the loose."

"That points to one killer."

"But David's murder was nothing like the others. He was shot, not strangled. He wasn't held prisoner, wasn't tied up and—most of all—he wasn't a young, blonde woman."

Earlier, Aiden had referred to a murder of opportunity. "What if David knew something about the serial murders? The killer would want him dead."

He turned toward her and gave her a long, hard stare. This scrutiny wasn't like his earlier friendly glances. He seemed to be looking deeper and with more concern. "You're a little too smart for your own good."

"I'm on to something, aren't I?"

"We found evidence of a connection," he said. "One of the deputies and I did a flyover in the

Spring Creek area where Ellen Jessop's body was found. We spotted tire tracks not far from the crime scene. The tread matched David's van."

Suddenly uncomfortable, she swallowed hard. Playing at investigation was fun. The idea of finding the truth about these terrible crimes was like turning over a rock and seeing a rattlesnake. "Do you think David was the serial killer?"

"There's a good chance his van was used by the killer. The sheriff took the vehicle to check it out, over the objections of Bert Welling who said the van belonged to him. There were blood traces inside. They'll be checking for a DNA match to Ellen."

As she stared through the windshield at the starlit skies, a horrible thought occurred. "David might have been following Misty because she was next on his list. But if David was the serial killer, who shot him?"

"Other people used that van," he said. "It was a kind of party bus."

The chopper hovered over her grandma's house, and Aiden turned on the spotlight in order to locate the best landing spot. She looked toward the lights of the nearby homes of the Martin and Tall Grass families, and Tab regretted the whirring noise of the rotors that would surely waken everybody inside and disturb their livestock.

"Why didn't you tell me about the tire tracks?" she demanded.

"I just told you everything I know."

"But I had to pry it out of you." He couldn't honestly claim that he'd been immediately forthcoming. "Were you trying to protect me again?"

"It didn't seem important." He eased the chopper into a smooth descent, constantly checking the ground below. "We can't pinpoint who used the van. The evidence isn't conclusive."

"And that comment about me being too smart. What did you mean by that?"

"Would you feel better if I said you were dumb?"

It wasn't like she was asking for a badge and a gun with a license to kill. She just wanted to be kept in the loop. He needed to trust her.

"Were you playing me?" she asked. "When you were asking questions about Connie, was that a ruse to keep from telling me about the investigation?"

The chopper touched down, and he turned off the engine before looking at her. "My interest in your work is genuine. I wasn't trying to trick you or divert your attention. I don't play games like that. I say what I mean."

In the light from the instrument panel, she studied the lines of his face, not allowing her thoughts to be diverted by the pleasing symmetry of his features. She knew he was an honest, responsible man, but he was also clever like the coyote in the stories her grandma used to tell when she was growing up. The coyote behaved in all kinds of unexplainable ways, getting the other animals to do his bidding. But there was almost always a moral to the story that showed the coyote was actually helping. Aiden was coyote clever but also good. And she knew he would never intentionally hurt her.

"I trust you," she said.

He reached toward her and lightly stroked her cheek. "That's all I can ask for."

"Let's gather up these things and get out of here."

He nodded toward Grandma's house. "The lights are on. Is that how you left the house?"

"I think so." When she and Grandma set out for the Gabriel ranch, it had been after dark. "Our neighbor, Sam Tall Grass, has been over here taking care of things."

"Does he have a key?"

"Grandma doesn't usually lock up." She swung open the chopper door. "We're so isolated out here that if somebody wants to break a window and get inside, there's not much to stop them."

He didn't have to lecture her about the need for security. Tab had spent most of her life in cities where doors were locked and deadbolts fastened. She climbed out of the chopper and headed toward the sweet little cabin that had been her grandma's home for as long as she could remember.

She liked to think that the house was protected by Grandma's reputation. Nobody wanted to get on the wrong side of Maria Spotted Bear. Still, Tab was reassured when she noticed that Aiden joined her on the porch, and she saw that he'd armed himself. He wore a holster at his hip.

He touched the butt of his gun. "Better safe than sorry."

"Agreed."

Inside the house, she sent Aiden to the kitchen to pick up Grandma's cooking supplies and put them into a cooler. Tab concentrated on the bedrooms, where she packed her clothes and those her grandma requested into two suitcases. Though tempted to take everything, she held back. Tomorrow or the next day, she'd be returning here to pick up Shua.

In a matter of minutes, she had the suitcases ready. As Aiden loaded them into the chopper, she checked the list her grandma had given him.

"Grandma's sneakers," she said with a groan. "I forgot them. I have to go back."

"Not a problem." He fell into step beside her. "I like the way your grandma's house smells."

"I know." The natural fragrance of the many herbs her grandma gathered and also cultivated mingled with years of baking and cooking. "If she could bottle that scent, she'd make a million dollars."

"I never thought your grandma was interested in money."

"That's cute, Aiden. Everybody needs more money." On the porch, she turned to him. "I'll run in and grab the shoes. You go to the horse barn, and I'll meet you there."

She didn't bother turning on lights as she hurried through the house. Tab knew where every chair and table was placed. In her grandma's bedroom, she knew she'd find the sneakers under the bed on the left side. Ducking down, she grabbed them.

When she stood, she looked directly at a window. She saw a shape outside the glass. Moonlight outlined the shoulders and head. Someone was out there. A man stood at the window, staring in at her.

Chapter Thirteen

Aiden had just stepped off the porch when he heard Tab yell his name. There was panic in her voice. She needed him.

He pivoted and ran back to the house, snatched the gun from his holster, dove inside. The lights were off. Turn them on? No, his eyes were already accustomed to the dark.

Tab burst from the hallway that led to the bedrooms. Her grandma's white sneakers were in her hands.

"I saw someone at the window," she said. "He ran off. Toward the barn."

"Did you see his face?"

"No. He had on a hoodie."

The threat was clear. An intruder had been waiting here. Waiting for Tab? Why, damn it, why? Aiden needed to catch this guy. At the same time, he had to protect Tab and couldn't leave her alone. His decision came quickly.

"Follow me," he said. "Stay close. If you hear gunfire, hit the ground."

Gun in hand, he charged out the door and ran toward a couple of scraggly pine trees between the house and barn. Adrenaline surged through him. His senses sharpened. Through the shadows, he saw movement. A man was running parallel to the corral fence, heading toward the horse barn.

"Stop," Aiden called out. "I'll shoot."

The man disappeared around the edge of the barn. From this distance, Aiden couldn't get any kind of description other than hooded sweatshirt and jeans. He didn't know if the intruder had entered the barn or not.

Likely, he'd gone through the side door. Why else would he have headed in that direction? At the front of the barn, he halted and turned to Tab, who stood close behind him. She wasn't even breathing hard. The woman really could run.

"How many entrances to the barn?" he asked.

"Three. The big double doors on the front and back, and the regular-size side door."

He didn't like the idea of rushing through the side door without knowing what he'd find on the other side. The intruder could be armed. He could be setting up an ambush, aiming his weapon at that door, prepared to shoot as soon as Aiden came though. From inside, he heard Shua give a nervous whinny.

Tab swore. "If he hurts my horse, I'll kill him."

Aiden went to the big double doors at the front and unfastened the latch. "When I open this door, want you to hide behind it. Stay low."

"I'm coming with you. That's my horse."

"No time to argue. I won't let him hurt Shua."

She stamped her foot once. Frustration was evident on her face. "Okay, I'll stay out here. But let me open the door. That leaves your hands free. Aiden, you've got to hurry."

The double doors were wide enough for a truck full of hay to pull inside. And they were heavy. As Tab grabbed the bar and pulled, he rushed inside and went to the left, ducking behind the edge of the first stall. A few bare bulbs cast a dim glow. Moonlight from the open door spilled onto the packed dirt floor. The side of the horse barn opposite the stalls was two stories tall with a hay loft above. The area below held rough work benches and racks for storing tack and other tools.

Aiden scanned the hay loft in the high part of the barn and listened for the sound of footsteps creaking in the rafters. He heard nothing, saw no sign of movement. If the intruder had climbed the ladder to the loft, he had the best vantage point. But it also meant that he was trapped; there was only one ladder.

Still keeping an eye on the loft, he peeked around the edge of his hiding place. Aiden counted four stalls with closed half doors. The farthest was occupied by Shua. The black horse poked his head through the half door and nickered. Nobody could have been hiding in the stall with the horse. Shua would have been more agitated.

A groan came from the stall beside him. Had the intruder injured himself? A rusty voice called out, "Help me."

Moving carefully but quickly, Aiden came around the edge of the stall and peered over the half door. Curled on the floor was a man with an arm outstretched. "Help me."

As soon as Aiden opened the half door and entered the stall, he was aware of movement at the far wall. The side door whipped open and cracked against the wall. The intruder was getting away, and there was nothing Aiden could do about it.

He wanted to give chase, but he couldn't abandon the person in distress. "Are you injured?"

The answer was a groan.

Aiden dropped to a squat and pulled aside the heavy buffalo robe. On his side with his shoulders hunched, Wally clutched the front of his blood-soaked shirt.

His wound looked more serious than anything Aiden could handle. Lucky for Wally, he had a nurse with him. "Tab," he called to her. "I need you."

In seconds, she appeared at the door of the stall.

"I saw the guy in the sweatshirt. He's running downhill, toward the road."

Even if Aiden could sprout wings and fly in pursuit, he wouldn't be able to catch the intruder and help Wally at the same time. "We're going to have to let him go."

She sank down beside him. Efficiently, she adjusted Wally's position so he was on his back.

The old man let out a groan. "It hurts."

Tab murmured words of assurance as she unbuttoned his shirt and pulled the fabric aside to get a better look at the wound on his upper chest. Breathing in frantic gasps, Wally clawed helplessly at her hands. His pale, scrawny chest heaved. His ribs stood out like a skeleton.

"He's been shot," Tab said. "I need a compress, something to hold against the wound to stop the bleeding."

"Do you have first-aid supplies in the house?"

"No time for that. We need to get him to a hospital. Give me your shirt."

Aiden stood and stripped down to his undershirt, which he whipped off and handed to her. As he put his shirt and jacket back on, he stared regretfully at the open door on the side of the barn where the intruder had escaped. Why had he lured them to the horse barn? He must have known they'd find Wally and help him. It didn't make sense unless he thought Wally was already dead.

Kneeling beside Tab, he grasped Wally's hand and leaned close to his face. The stink from the old man was beyond disgusting. "Wally, can you hear me?"

His eyes wavered wildly. "Am I going to die?"

"You're going to be all right," Tab said. "We're going to take you to the hospital in the chopper."

To her, he said, "You told me I could visit Maria Spotted Bear. You said I could come here. Anytime."

"It's okay. I'm not angry."

"Anytime, you said so."

Tab placed Aiden's white undershirt against the still-bleeding wound. "This will hurt. I'm going to apply pressure to stop the bleeding. Do you have any other injuries?"

"On my noggin. I think he hit me."

"Who hit you?" Aiden asked. "Did you get a look at him?"

"He was a two-face."

"What?"

Tab grabbed his hand and placed it over his now-ruined undershirt. "I want you to keep applying pressure."

"What's a 'two-face'?"

Ignoring him, she spoke to Wally. "Can you sit up? I want to look at your head."

"A two-face," Wally repeated. "Never look him

in the eye. He'll freeze your bones down to the marrow."

Though Aiden had no idea what he was babbling about, Aiden played along. "Did the two-face say anything?"

"Said I saw too much. Talked too much."

"Enough," Tab said. "Wally, try to sit up."

With her help, Wally dragged himself off the floor and immediately slumped forward. Dark blood matted the hair on the back of his head. His shoulders heaved. He began to wheeze.

"He might have a punctured lung," Tab said. "Do you have a gurney or spine board in the chopper?"

"Both." Wally's cough convulsed his entire body. He didn't look good. "But it's going to take a while for me to get them unpacked. Is there time?"

"He's lost a lot of blood. I don't see an exit wound, which means the bullet is still in him. The sooner we can get him to the hospital, the better."

"I'll carry him."

"It's not the best procedure. The blow to his head might have caused spinal or neck injury."

He understood her concerns and her medical professionalism, but if they didn't get Wally to immediate care, he might not make it. This was an emergency situation. Proper procedure didn't apply.

"I'm taking him." Aiden slapped his gun into her hand. "If somebody comes after us, don't hesitate to open fire."

He wrapped the buffalo robe around the old man and lifted him like a child into his arms. He didn't weigh much, but carrying him was clumsy. His old hands folded in against his chest. When his eyes closed, he looked half dead.

"Careful," Tab said. "Don't trip."

"Trying not to."

They left the horse barn and went past the house. Balancing Wally in his arms, Aiden got into a regular rhythm. As he strode toward the chopper, he heard that old song in his head. *He ain't heavy, he's my brother.* The Buffalo Man wasn't family or even a close friend, but Aiden cared about what happened to the old guy. *He ain't heavy. He ain't heavy.*

At the chopper, Tab opened the rear door and jumped inside. She pulled a padded gurney down from the wall where it had been stowed. Aiden stretched Wally out on the padding. As he released his hold, the old man reached up and grabbed his arm.

Wheezing and gasping, he managed to choke out one word. "Goodbye."

"You're not leaving," Aiden said. "We're in this together. You and me and Tab."

In minutes, the helicopter was airborne. Using the emergency frequency, he contacted St. John's Hospital in Billings to let the E.R. know that he was bringing in a gunshot victim. There was a closer facility in Henley, but they weren't as well equipped and didn't have a helipad. The extra ten minutes to get to Billings was worth the risk for better surgeons and better possibility for transfusion.

Looking over his shoulder, he watched Tab administer first aid with bandages and supplies from a well-stocked rescue kit. "Hey," he called back to her. "How's he doing?"

"Resting." She spoke loudly over the sound of the rotors. "Having trouble breathing."

He held the headset toward her. "I've got the E.R. at St. John's on the line. Tell them what you need."

As soon as she had the headset in place, Tab started rattling off medical jargon that sounded like a foreign language to him. Though triage wasn't her specialty, Tab knew what she was doing. Her competence impressed him. Her cool courage amazed him.

Under pressure, she had performed like a champ. Nobody could have done better. He might have to rethink his objections to having her on his team. She was decisive and efficient. When he'd told her to stay hidden, she'd agreed without too much hesitation. When he'd needed her help, she was there.

After she finished talking to the docs, she left Wally and came forward to stand behind him in the cockpit. "How much longer?"

"Fifteen or twenty minutes."

She gripped his shoulder and squeezed. "I think he's going to make it."

He looked up into her beautiful eyes. There was so much he wanted to tell her, but now wasn't the time. "I'm glad we got to him in time."

"He's a tough old guy. The bullet wound and the blow to the head would have killed most people."

"That has to be what the intruder was thinking. He wouldn't want us to find Wally alive."

"That ugly old buffalo robe might have saved his life by keeping him warm so he didn't go into shock."

Wally's survival was the most important thing, but Aiden had to wonder about what the old man had witnessed. He knew something that made him a threat. "Do you know what he meant by a 'two-face'?"

"It's a monster used to scare kids. You know how it goes, clean your room or two-face will eat you."

"Somehow, I can't imagine your grandma using that kind of threat."

"She never had to. She's got an angry glare that always made me toe the line."

"Tell me more about two-face."

"He's a huge ogre with one face in front and another in back so you can never sneak away from him. And he has claws like a grizzly, I think. If you're naughty, he'll come after you. First, he freezes you with an evil eye. Then, he eats you, starting with your toes."

That was all they needed—a flesh-eating ogre.

"When Wally comes around, he might be able to give us a better identification. What do you think he really saw?"

"Somebody wearing a ski mask?"

Good guess. He'd seen ski masks designed with monster faces or skull heads. If somebody came at Wally wearing one of those, he might think he'd seen a monster.

Tab leaned closer and brushed her lips against his cheek. Her kiss was so soft and so quick that he wasn't even sure it happened. But he felt her nearness.

"I'm so proud of you," she said.

"Why? I let the bad guy escape."

"The way you picked Wally up and carried him was so terrific. You saw what had to be done, and you did it."

"Anybody else would have done the same. Carrying him wasn't hard." He grinned up at her. "He ain't heavy. He's my brother."

"And you're my hero."

After another squeeze to his shoulder, she returned to the rear of the chopper to tend to her patient while Aiden basked in the glow of her praise. He'd done plenty of emergency rescues and evacuations, but nothing felt as satisfying as this moment. Her appreciation meant the world to him.

As soon as they touched down, he needed to contact Sheriff Fielding and arrange for Wally to be guarded against another attack while he was in the hospital. The old man knew something or had witnessed an event that he didn't realize was important. And the killer had come after him to make sure he didn't talk. That was the only explanation that made sense. If Wally could remember what he had witnessed, he might be key to breaking open the investigation.

It worried Aiden that the attack had taken place at Maria Spotted Bear's house. A coincidence? In his babbling, Wally seemed to be telling Tab that he'd come to the house because of her invitation. Had the killer been following Wally and tracked him to the house? Or was he already there, waiting and watching?

Tab was also a witness. She'd seen the face at the window. Had he been coming for her?

It was a damn good thing that she and her grandma were staying at the ranch. Tab needed protection. From this moment forward, Aiden wouldn't leave her alone and unguarded. Not for a moment.

Chapter Fourteen

The next day, Tab didn't wake until sunlight was streaking through the window blinds in her upstairs bedroom at the ranch. Something was wrong with her foot. She kicked and pried her eyelids all the way open. Misty was sitting on the edge of the bed by Tab's bare feet.

"Brought you coffee, toast and a banana," Misty said.

"What time is it?"

"After ten o'clock."

"Were you pinching my toes?"

"A little bit." Misty pushed herself upright and waddled to the bedside table where she'd placed a tray with the breakfast. "I thought you'd want to be up. You were always an early riser."

If anybody else had been bugging her to rise and shine after the super-strenuous day she'd had yesterday, Tab would have growled for them to go away and snuggled deeper into the warm covers. But she had a soft spot for Misty. Ten years ago, in this very bedroom, they'd giggled and whispered and tried on lipstick. Rearranging the pillows so she could lean against them, Tab reached for the mug of hot black coffee.

After a sip, she studied Misty and decided that this toe-pinching wake-up call didn't really have anything to do with her. Misty had something to say, and she'd chosen Tab as her confidante.

Cautiously, Tab asked, "How are you feeling this morning?"

"I'm okay." She giggled. "The baby is even better, doing jumping jacks inside my belly."

"Aiden said you wanted me to deliver your baby. Is that true?"

"Will you? Please say yes. I want to have my baby here at the ranch."

Tab would check with her doctor to make sure there were no complications that might require hospitalization, but she didn't expect problems. "I'd be happy to deliver the next generation of the Gabriel family."

"All right."

Misty did a double fist pump that reminded Tab of yesterday's unfortunate football metaphor. "You were a cheerleader, weren't you?"

"Head cheerleader."

Tab figured that Misty had sailed through high school as one of the popular kids. She was pretty and smart and her family had money. "Prom queen?"

"Junior prom and senior homecoming queen." Her giggle fell flat. "By senior prom, everybody knew I was pregnant. I wasn't showing or anything, but they knew. They treated me different, like my life was over or something."

Living a charmed existence and then having it taken away had to be difficult. Was that what Misty wanted to talk about? Her prospects for the future?

Tab picked up the plate with heavily buttered toast smeared with homemade chokecherry jelly. Taking a bite, she considered what to say next. She wanted to encourage Misty without sounding pushy or preachy. "Your life isn't over. It's just beginning."

"Yeah, yeah, I know. That's what Aiden says, too." She sat on the edge of the bed again. "He says that even with a baby, I can still go to college or law school or whatever."

Her eye-rolling attitude showed an almost total indifference to this topic. What was Misty after? Tab didn't have the patience for a guessing game. "You woke me up because you want to talk about something. What is it?"

"It's Clinton," she said. "We had a really big fight yesterday and it was kind of your fault. Because you talked to him and told him he made a smart deduction."

"Don't you think he's smart?"

"Sure, I do. When we're alone and he's not showing off, he's got a lot to say. And he's creative. He writes songs for me and the baby."

"That's sweet." The more Tab found out about Clinton, the more she liked him.

"But now he thinks he can figure out who the killer is, and that's stupid. Look what happened when he went and talked to Ellen about my wristwatch. Clinton ended up being a suspect."

Though Tab had been pushing Aiden to let her participate in his investigative process, she had to agree with Misty. Clinton could say the wrong thing to the wrong person and end up in serious trouble. "What was he planning to do?"

"For starters, he was going to talk to Chuck and Woody. He thinks they know something." She gave an unladylike snort. "Those two toads are lucky to remember their own names."

Still, the toads would be more willing to talk to Clinton than the sheriff. "Did he do it?"

"I don't know." Her concern was evident in the lack of giggling, smirking and eye rolling. "I haven't seen Clinton today, and we usually meet up the minute he comes to work."

"You've had no contact at all?"

"A text message at seven o'clock this morning. It said 'Luv U.' I called, and he won't answer his phone."

"Try sending him a text."

While Misty wrote her message, Tab finished off

the toast and the coffee. Misty was right to worry about Clinton, especially after the assault on Wally. Playing games with a serial killer was like yanking a tiger's tail. The beast could turn and bite.

"Done," Misty said.

"I think we should tell Aiden."

"Not yet. I don't want to give him another reason to hate my boyfriend. Speaking of boyfriends…" Her giggle returned. "What's going on with you and my brother?"

"What makes you think there's something? Are you in on this matchmaking thing with your mom and my grandma?"

"I see how he looks at you. He likes you, Tab."

It took all her self-control not to join in the giggles and start gushing. "We're friends. That's all."

"We'll just see about that." Misty tapped a contact number on her phone. "He told me to call as soon as you were awake."

"Now? You're calling him now?"

"The perfect time."

"Give me that phone." Tab made a grab, but pregnant Misty was surprisingly quick.

She hopped off the bed and spoke into her phone. "Tab wants to see you. She's still in bed."

Tab panicked. Her long hair hung around her face in witchy strands. Her blue, cotton nightshirt was only as long as her knees, and the fabric was too thin and clingy. Looking down, she noticed a huge black-and-blue bruise on her forearm, which she must have gotten when struggling to treat Wally. And her teeth weren't brushed. And she had to pee. And the bathroom was down the hall. She didn't want Aiden to see her like this.

But he was already knocking at the door. "Can I come in?"

"No!" Tab yelled.

Misty opened the door and ushered her brother inside. Sweetly, she said, "I'll leave you two alone." And she closed the door behind her.

Tab pulled the covers up to her chin. "I'm not awake."

"I can leave, but I thought you might want an update on Wally."

"Well, yes." And she was acting like a dope. There was no reason for her to be embarrassed. They were only friends, right? She cleared her throat, lifted her chin and said, "Tell me about Wally."

He dragged a chair from the matching pine desk, placed it by the bed and straddled it. "Since last night, his condition has been upgraded to critical but stable. The doctors sound confident about his recovery."

"That's a relief."

She wasn't surprised. Last night, they'd waited until the surgery was complete and the doctors gave them a positive prognosis. Wally's organ damage was limited to a collapsed lung, which was serious but not life-threatening. He had no broken bones. His concussion would bear watching, but there was no bleeding in the brain. The worst problem was a heavy loss of blood from the wounds.

"The docs also said that your first-aid compress to slow the bleeding probably saved his life."

"I can't take all the credit," she said. "There were a couple of bloody rags in the stall with Wally. He must have tried a compress of his own."

"Does that mean I sacrificed my undershirt in vain?"

"Not at all." She'd gotten a very nice view of his bare chest. "It means Wally started his own first aid before we came on the scene. Has he been awake?"

"A couple of times," Aiden said. "The police in Billings have a man posted at his bed to make sure he stays safe."

"Have they been able to ask any questions?"

"They've tried but haven't gotten any coherent answers. According to Wally, a two-face monster attacked him."

To avoid looking at him, she burrowed more deeply under the navy-blue comforter. When she spoke, her voice was muffled. "I wish we knew what happened to him."

"The doctor had a theory. Want to hear it?"

"Yes."

"Would you come out from under the covers? I feel like I'm talking to a navy blue lump."

"I told you I was still asleep." She slanted a glance toward him. His hands rested on the back of the chair and his chin rested on his hands. His eyes were trained on her, and she didn't want to face him. "If you don't like it, you can—"

"Fine," he said. "According to the doc, Wally was shot twice in the back at close range. One of the bullets lodged inside, and the other went all the way through."

"The injury on his chest was from an exit wound," she said. "That's why it bled so much."

"It also explains why Wally isn't dead. The shots were aimed at his heart, but the angle of his body meant the bullets went high. The doctor thought Wally might have been on the ground, crawling to get away."

"The killer must have hit him in the back of the head. Then Wally went down. While he was attempting to crawl away, the shots were fired."

She hated to imagine the old man in his buffalo robe fleeing from a stone-cold killer. Wally must have been terrified and confused. No wonder he couldn't remember anything.

Her grip on the covers loosened. Her embarrassment about her messy hair and lack of hygiene were petty problems when compared to the attack on Wally. It was time for her to grow up. "If we hadn't found him when we did…"

"He wouldn't have survived."

"It almost seems like the killer led us directly to him."

"That's been bothering me," he said. "He must have thought Wally was already dead. Leading us to the barn was a bit of misdirection because his car was parked the other way."

Turning her head, she looked directly at Aiden. He was shaved and showered, neatly dressed in a plaid shirt and jeans. His combed brown hair made her acutely aware of the tangled mess on her head. She reached up to shove a chunk of hair off her forehead.

"Your arm," he said, "what happened?"

"I don't remember when I bruised it. It must have been when I was struggling with Wally."

Gently, he took her arm and studied the ugly mark above her wrist. His hands were cold from being outside. "Does it hurt?"

"Not really."

Her gaze met his, and she sank into the depths of his cool gray eyes. In the facets, she saw flecks of forest green and pure silver, a mesmerizing combination of dark and light. She couldn't stop staring.

Their position should have felt more intimate. She was in bed, after all. If she encouraged him, he might be tempted to lie beside her. But there was no way she'd cuddle when she had to go to the bathroom. Kissing with her unbrushed teeth was absolutely out of the question.

She snatched her arm from his grasp. "What else have you been doing this morning?"

"Talking to the law." He resettled himself in the chair. "Early this morning, Joseph Lefthand went to your grandma's house to investigate. He didn't see any sign of a break-in, but he found a blood trail in the barn that seemed to indicate Wally was shot there and then crawled into the horse stall. And he pulled some fingerprints that he's sending to the sheriff for identification."

"Good for Joseph Lefthand. What about Sheriff Fielding?"

"His new favorite theory, based on the tire tracks from David's van near the dump site for Ellen's body, is that David was the serial killer but wasn't working alone."

"He's not still considering a gang, is he?"

"Now, he thinks there were just two of them. David had a partner, and this partner killed him and attacked Wally."

"That's good news for Misty. It means the sheriff doesn't suspect her anymore."

"I'm just not sure that it's the truth," Aiden said. "I've heard of dual serial killers before. Usually, one is dominant and the other does his bidding."

From the little they knew about David, she

doubted he'd be the boss. As a child, David had been shuttled back and forth between his alcoholic father and his strict uncle Bert. His unrequited crush on Misty seemed immature. Aiden called it stalking, but she thought David was one of those guys who drove past his supposed girlfriend's house and sent her unwanted gifts.

She remembered the story Misty had told about her encounter with David. He seemed easily manipulated. A con man like Aspen Jim would be quick to take advantage of someone like David.

But it wasn't really fair for her to draw these kinds of conclusions. Tab had never spoken to David. Though she'd probably seen him around town, she'd never noticed him.

"It's hard to know what's true," she said.

"And there's not much in the way of evidence." He swung his leg off the chair and stood. "What are your plans for the day?"

"I want to check up on Connie and Carlos and baby Rosalie. Other than that, I'm free."

"Tell me when you want to go. I'll drive."

Keeping herself covered, she sat up on the bed. "I don't remember inviting you along."

"I'm going to stick close to you, Tab. Until we're 100 percent sure that the killer wasn't lurking around at your grandma's house, waiting to attack you, I'm your bodyguard."

"Why me?"

"You were a witness to David's murder."

Before she could object, he left the bedroom. When he went out the door, the sunlight dimmed and the room felt empty. Her friendship with Aiden was on the verge of becoming something more, and she was anxious to see what came next.

Chapter Fifteen

After lunch, Aiden, Tab and Misty were on their
way to the little house on the outskirts of Henley
where Connie and Carlos lived. Aiden rode shot-
gun in Tab's van, an appropriate seating arrangement given his claim to be her bodyguard.

Earlier, when he announced that plan, he'd expected her to launch into one of her tirades about
being able to take care of herself. Instead, she'd
ducked under the covers and hadn't complained
a bit. Damn, she was complicated—shy but confident, funny and serious at the same time, kind-
hearted with others but demanding when it came to
herself. She'd picked up street smarts from living
in cities, but he knew she would always be rooted
in the traditions of her people. Figuring out Tab
Willows might be a lifetime project.

His agenda for now was to make sure she was
safe. And he'd taken precautions. After explaining the potential danger to Blake, they cut back
the daily chores to the bare minimum and put the

men on high alert. Every ranch hand was armed and they rotated in shifts doing guard duty, patrolling near the main house and barns on horseback with rifles. Protecting the herd that was spread out over several acres a couple of miles from here would have been impossible without an army, but the cattle weren't under threat. Danger from the serial killer was aimed at Tab and maybe Misty. And Aiden had it covered.

Being a passenger in her van gave him the opportunity to sit back in his seat and study her as she drove. This afternoon, she looked fresh scrubbed and neat with her raven hair pulled back in a glossy braid. Her blue wool jacket brought out the color of her eyes. His gaze measured the angle of her cheekbones, the stubborn thrust of her jaw and her long, graceful neck. Was it possible for a throat to be beautiful? He was fascinated by the hollow at the base of her throat. She was wearing a necklace with a four-leaf clover pendant, which he recognized right away.

He'd given her that pendant ten years ago, a silly little gift to let her know he was grateful for the way she was handling Misty. She'd kept it all these years. That must mean something.

She shot him a questioning look. "You're staring."

"Am I?"

"Oh, yeah," said Misty from the backseat. "You've

been totally checked out, haven't been listening to a word I said."

"Did I miss anything important?"

"You're such a jerk, Aiden." His little sister huffed and giggled at the same time. "Tab, are you sure it's okay for us to visit?"

"When I called Connie, she said the more the merrier. And there was background noise so I think she has other visitors. How could she not want to see us? We're bringing two of Grandma's pies and your baby gift."

"The cutest baby snowsuit, pink with fake fur. I got it in Billings."

Aiden asked, "Weren't you saving that for your baby?"

"I'd rather let Connie have it," Misty said. "I'm really happy for her. Do you think she'll let me hold little Rosalie?"

"That's up to her," Tab said. "But I think she will."

"Since we both will have babies the same age, I know we're going to be really good friends. We can do play dates together and share babysitting."

"Glad you see it that way," Tab said. "It takes a village, you know."

She parallel parked on the street outside a small frame house with flower beds that would be colorful in the spring and a small crab apple tree to the left of the sidewalk. Carlos worked at the tree nursery, and Aiden had always thought he had talent in landscaping.

In addition to two cars in the concrete driveway, three other vehicles were parked on the street behind them. He wasn't surprised that Connie had plenty of visitors. She was a popular waitress at the local café, and she knew everybody. The whole town had been watching Connie's belly grow and taking bets on when she'd pop. But he hadn't expected to see Bert Welling. The gas station owner, still dressed in his spotless gray jumpsuit, came out the door as they approached.

Aiden gave him a nod. "Hi, Bert. I didn't know you were interested in babies."

"I'm not." His stern mouth pulled into a frown. "But Connie takes good care of me at the café. Every morning for breakfast, she serves me two eggs sunny-side up, four slices of bacon and wheat toast, buttered light. I'm good to people who are good to me."

"And those who aren't?"

The frown deepened. "See you around, Aiden."

As he went down the sidewalk, he acknowledged Tab and Misty with a slight nod of his head, but he didn't say a word to them. Aiden had to wonder if Bert was aware of his nephew's attraction to Misty. Did he ever talk to David? Did he know anything of that young man's hopes and dreams? It was hard to tell if Bert thought of his nephew as someone who was good to him or as a problem he had to deal with.

Following Tab and Misty into the house, Aiden watched for reaction from the other townspeople. If Chuck and Woody could be used as an example, lots of folks would be blaming his sister for David's murder. In addition to Connie and Carlos, there were four other people who greeted them. They all seemed friendly. One bland, middle-aged lady who worked as a teacher at the high school gave Misty a giant hug and remarked about how awful it must have been to see David killed.

"It was terrible," Misty said.

He didn't trust his sister to keep quiet about the murder. "She's not at liberty to talk about what happened. That's Sheriff Fielding's order. We're here to celebrate this pretty new baby."

Standing beside the rocking chair where Connie was sitting, he leaned down to get a better look at the tiny bundle in her arms. Sound asleep, Rosalie held one perfect little hand beside her Cupid's bow mouth. Aiden felt a tug at his heart. "She's the prettiest baby I've ever seen."

Connie beamed. "She has black hair, like her daddy."

"But Carlos isn't this cute." He glanced toward the proud papa. "No offense, man."

"None taken. I want my baby girl to look just like her mama."

Tab stood on the opposite side of the rocking chair. "How has she been with the breastfeeding?"

"It's just like you told me," Connie said. "Every three hours or so, she's hungry. And my boobs have turned into milking machines."

"Too much information," Aiden said.

"Get used to it," Tab warned. "You're going to have one of these at your house very soon."

He liked the idea, but he was a little bit scared, as well. "Every three hours?"

"Not your problem," Tab said. "I know you're the most responsible person in the world, but breast feeding is Misty's job."

He stepped aside to let Misty take his place. Though she cooed and giggled over the baby, he saw a subtle transformation in his sister. She seemed calmer and less focused on herself. An immediate bond formed between her and Connie as they talked about babies and childbirth.

While Tab took Connie and Carlos into a bedroom to talk about other things, he and Misty milled around with the other people. Their interactions stayed upbeat and pleasant, appropriate for celebrating a new birth. Still, there were occasional references to the terrible serial killings and the murder of Ellen Jessop. A hint of fear whispered below the surface of their conversations. A terrible danger threatened their community.

The serene atmosphere changed when Woody

and Chuck appeared at the door. Before Carlos showed them inside, Aiden intervened. "If you don't mind, I'd like to talk to these two outside for a moment."

Carlos looked from one to the other. "You all play nice. I don't want fighting around my daughter."

Outside on the sidewalk, Aiden squared his shoulders. "Like Carlos said, I don't want any trouble."

"We get it." Chuck spoke through pinched lips. His tone was hostile. "And if we don't behave, you'll chase us down with your chopper and have us thrown in jail."

After shooting off guns near his house, they deserved to be arrested. Aiden wouldn't apologize for the role he played. "If that's what it takes, then so be it."

Inhaling a deep breath, Chuck pushed out his chest. "My mom told me I had to say I was sorry."

"Not necessary," Aiden responded. "Just don't do it again."

Woody hadn't said a word. He stared down at his boots. In his hands, he held a couple of pieces of loose twine that he kept fiddling with. Instead of his Bronco jersey, he wore a neat blue windbreaker shirt and jeans that made Aiden think he'd also had a talk with his mother. These two young men were out of high school, but their parents were still an influence in their lives.

Woody looked up. "Is Misty here?"

She stepped outside and closed the door behind her. "I'm right here. If there's something you want to say, tell me to my face."

Aiden had never been so proud of his sister. Even pregnant, she was showing more guts than these two guys who accused her in a nasty note and ran away.

"We were wrong," Woody said.

"You were," she said. "What made you do it?"

"We were mad about David getting himself killed."

"I don't buy it." There were no giggles from Misty. "You guys weren't that close to David. You worked with him at the gas station, but you didn't hang out with him much. You thought you were better than him because you were jocks."

"We're sorry," Chuck said. "Okay? Can that be an end to it?"

"Why did you come after me? Who were you talking to?"

Woody opened his mouth but Chuck spoke first. "Nobody, we weren't talking to nobody."

She took a step toward them with her belly protruding aggressively. "It was Jim, wasn't it? That lame-brain ski bum who thinks he's all that." She snapped her fingers in Chuck's face. "Aspen Jim is nothing but a phony."

"You're not going to say that when he opens Little Big Horn Rafting Company. We're going to be the first guys he hires."

"That's right." Woody held up the piece of rope he'd been playing with. "I'm learning knots so I know how to handle the rafts."

Or tie up helpless victims? Aiden had to wonder what other actions Aspen Jim had demanded from them. He didn't see Chuck and Woody as killers; they were basically decent and still respected their parents...if that was any kind of alibi.

He was amazed by how much information his sister had gotten in a short, angry confrontation. In jail, the sheriff had questioned Chuck and Woody extensively and hadn't learned that they were acting on something Aspen Jim had told them. Apparently, the only way to break the teenage code of silence was through another teenager.

Misty braced her hands on her hips. "Here's what I want you to tell Jim. If he's got a problem with me, he can bring it to me himself. Just bring it."

"Whoa." Woody held up his hands to fend off her rage. "The Gabriel family is real kickass."

"You better believe it," Misty said.

"Is it okay if we go in and see the baby now?" Chuck asked. "My mom told me I had to say hi to

Connie. After being in jail, I've got to prove I'm not some kind of criminal."

"One more question," Aiden said. "Aspen Jim convinced you that Misty had something to do with David's murder. Who changed your mind?"

"Clinton," they said in unison. "He was there. He ought to know what really went down."

"When did you see him?" Misty asked.

"Yesterday afternoon. He's a good guy, Misty. You're lucky to be with him."

"I know."

For once, Aiden agreed with her about Clinton. He'd taken on the task of convincing people that Misty was innocent. Aiden had to respect him for that.

ALL DAY LONG AIDEN HAD kept to his promise to watch over Tab. They'd done everything together, from a trip into Billings to check up on the Buffalo Man to helping out in the kitchen with dinner. But the day was winding to an end, and he'd have to leave her alone to sleep. Or not…

The best way for him to protect her would be to have her lying beside him in his bed. All day long, they had been touching, occasionally holding hands and exchanging long, lingering gazes. Their closeness sent his imagination into overdrive. When he leaned close and caught a whiff of her shampoo, he'd fantasize about kissing the nape of her neck, rowning in the delicate scent from her hair. Every esture she made seemed like a caress. The sound f her laughter was sexy. Her sighs penetrated his oul.

Too bad their lovemaking was only in his head. Ie wanted to separate her from the rest of his family and get her alone in his cabin, but that didn't eem to be happening. After dinner, he and Tab at in the living room with his mom and Blake nd Misty. Maria Spotted Bear had already gone pstairs to bed, but the rest of the crew seemed as f they could spend the whole damn night talking.

"We saw my dad in Billings," Tab said. "He says ello to everyone."

"I've always liked your father," Sylvia said. When Aiden built his cabin a couple of years ago, e tried to hire your dad to do it. But he was too usy."

"Not many building contractors have been as uccessful as my dad. He doesn't do much in the vay of new construction, but he has four different rews working on renovations and repairs."

Sylvia nudged Blake in the ribs. "We could use ome renovating around here."

"I want to fix up the old bunkhouse," Misty said.

Aiden slouched lower in his chair. This was an ld argument from Misty. A couple of years back, t the same time Aiden was building his cabin, hey'd constructed a new bunkhouse for the crew that lived full time at the ranch. Instead of tearing down the old barracks, they used it for storage Misty had a different plan. She wanted to turn the old bunkhouse into her own little home for herself and the baby.

She giggled and chattered away about how easy it would be to make the renovations. This afternoon, when she saw how happy Connie and Carlos were, she must have started rethinking her plan to raise her baby alone because she spent the entire drive back to the ranch talking about Clinton.

"I'd like to see it," Tab said.

He hadn't been following the conversation. "See what?"

"Your cabin." Her blue eyes confronted him. "I've seen it from the outside, but I'd like to check out the interior."

He didn't need further invitation. Aiden jumped to his feet. "I'd be happy to show you around."

As they left the main house, he clasped her hand. *This might turn out to be a good night, after all.*

Chapter Sixteen

Once again, Tab was holding hands with Aiden and walking the familiar route from the main house toward the barn. But this time was different. They weren't racing toward the chopper to pursue a bad guy or to visit the hospital. She was on her way to the special place he'd built to give himself privacy—on her way to his house with his living room, his dining room, his kitchen and his bedroom.

She still couldn't believe that she'd invited herself. Asking if she could see his home? That little ruse hadn't fooled anybody. Tab had seen the knowing look that passed between Sylvia and Blake. Misty had been smiling so hard that Tab thought for a moment that the perky little blonde would whip out her cheerleader pom-poms, pregnant or not.

Everybody seemed to want a relationship to work out between her and Aiden. This afternoon, her dad had come right out and asked if they were dating,

and he'd looked disappointed when she told hir
they were just friends.

Maybe that was the truth. Maybe they weren
meant to be anything more than pals. Or mayb
she needed to take a risk and let him get close. He
hand, held firmly in his grasp, began to sweat.

"I wish we'd had more time with your dad,
Aiden said. "During that summer when you wer
babysitting, I talked to him a lot, and he had goo
advice."

Her dad was a quiet man who usually kept hi
thoughts to himself. When he spoke, he was wortl
listening to. "What did he tell you?"

"That summer when my dad died was hell. Mor
could barely get out of bed. Misty kept a smile or
her little face, but I could see she was hurting."

"So were you."

"Mostly, I was overwhelmed. The business o
running the ranch kept piling up, and I didn't knov
what the hell I was doing. Outside contractors trie
to take advantage of me because I wasn't as savv
as my dad. Half the ranch hands were fixing t
quit. I didn't know who I should trust and who
should fire."

She'd been aware of those pressures, but mostl
she'd been consumed by how handsome he was
"You did a good job of hiding how you felt."

"I couldn't let anybody know that I was in ove
my head and drowning. But your dad saw the truth

and he gave me two pieces of advice. The first thing he said was that it was natural for me to be mad at my father for leaving me with this mess. I had to let that anger out. And you know what? He was right. I remember going for long walks with my dog, and when I was far away and alone, I'd just stand and yell, cursing so loud I could have raised the dead."

On the night she'd decided he was the perfect man, he must have been returning from one of those sessions. "I knew you took night walks with Reilly."

"Don't get me wrong. I don't blame my father for dying. He loved life, loved his life on the ranch. But I was so damn mad at what his death did to me." He gave her hand a squeeze. "Can you guess the second piece of advice from your dad?"

"He told you that there's no shame in asking for help," she said. "That's kind of his mantra."

"It's what you said to me when you were talking about helping me investigate. And you were right. I don't know what I would have done with Wally if you hadn't been there."

"We're good together."

"I reckon we are."

Her comment wasn't meant to be suggestive, but it sounded like it was. Good together? As in good in bed together? Her tension was rising. Though the night was cool, she was on fire. More sweat gathered at her hairline, and a drop trickled between her breasts. Her hands were practically dripping.

As they rounded the barn, she faked a stumble and pulled her hand away from him. She rubbed her palm on her jeans. "Clumsy me."

"Are you all right?"

Admitting that she was nervous wouldn't be smart—he'd want to know why. And she didn't want to tell him that she was expecting more than a tour of his living space. "Sure, I'm fine."

As long as they continued to talk about the past she could maintain her self-control, and she desperately wanted to keep that distance. "Do you remember my mom?"

"The beautiful Emma Willows, you bet I remember. I was only ten or eleven when she died, and it was one of the saddest days of my life. She and my mom were good friends. And I remember you were an annoying little pest."

"Me?" She might have gone back too far in time.

"You were a lot younger than me, and you were female. At that time, I didn't want anything to do with girls. No tea parties. No dressing up. No fancy-pants games."

They walked past the gleaming-white helicopter. His house was close enough to see clearly in the moonlight and the glow of a porch light that must have been on a timer. Though his house had wood siding like most of the other buildings on the anch, the architecture was more modern with an A-frame center section and many more windows. She stumbled again, this time for real. She wasn't ready to go inside.

"Tell me about my mom," she said.

"She had black hair like you, only she didn't wear it as long. And she smiled a lot more than you do. I remember that she loved dancing. She and my mom played the radio while they were in the kitchen, and they always ended up dancing around. So did you, twirling in circles."

"I danced?"

"Don't you remember?"

"My memories of my mom aren't clear. Mostly, I look at photos and make up stories to go along with the picture."

"You were young," he said.

They had reached the steps leading to a large deck that ran across the front and north side. The picnic table and the monster-size gas grill suggested that this was a great place for parties. Easily, she imagined a group of people drinking beer, cooking steaks and sitting around the kitchen table. She hadn't really met his friends. Everybody knew Aiden, but she didn't know who he hung out with.

She followed him up the stairs to the deck and caught hold of his arm. "It's such a pretty night. Can we stay out here? I'd like to hear more about your memories of my mother."

"Have a seat." He gestured to the picnic table. "I'll just step inside and grab a beer. Want one?"

"Sure." She wasn't much of a drinker. The studies linking Native Americans and alcoholism acted as an effective deterrent, but she liked the taste of beer.

When he opened a sliding glass door and turned on a light, she had a view of the interior kitchen with granite counters and stainless-steel appliances. She actually was curious to see his furnishings, but that wasn't the real reason she was here.

By staying outside, she postponed the inevitable moment when they would either make love or decide to be friends only. She wasn't sure which alternative scared her more. Though she'd dated plenty of men, her relationships never went deep.

She sat on the picnic table with her feet resting on the bench and took the beer when he returned. He climbed onto the table beside her. "What do you want to know about your mom?"

"I know she and your mom went to the ballet when your mom visited us in Billings. What else did they do together?"

"Watched chick flicks. Back then, it was VCR tapes from the video store in Henley." He tilted his beer to his mouth. "They baked cakes and breads, and tried out new recipes that made me gag. When they decorated for holidays, they always made sure you and me were involved. Since your mom was an artist, the decorating was always a treat. My mom still has some Easter eggs that your mom painted."

It pleased her to know that the Gabriel family had such fond remembrances of her mom. Those good feelings seeped into her consciousness and relaxed her. She inhaled a deep breath and exhaled. The night was still. From a faraway meadow, she heard the lowing of cattle.

Her life would have been different if her mom hadn't died when she was so young. Her dad and grandma had done a good job raising her, always supporting her and making her feel loved, but she missed the advice of a mother, especially when it came to men. Her father taught her to be suspicious of the guys she dated, and he'd never talked to her about sex. Though Grandma was more open-minded, she nursed the hope that someday Tab might marry into the tribe. What did it mean that Grandma was matchmaking with Aiden? Had she decided that Tab better marry soon before she became a dried-up old maid?

Turning her head, she met Aiden's gaze. The vibrant sensations coursing through her were far from withered. She took a long pull from her beer. She had to act or explode.

"I'm ready to go inside."

His touch as he helped her down from her perch sent a jolt of electricity across the surface of her skin. The same voltage shocked her when he rested his hand on the small of her back and directed her through the sliding glass doors. The hairs on her arms trembled as he helped her off with her jacket and hung it on a peg by the door.

As he strolled through the kitchen, he pointed out the major features and appliances. The narrative continued into the adjoining dining room, but she was too preoccupied to listen. Vaguely, she registered that this was a modern design with a spacious living room that rose two stories to the peak of the A-frame.

"It's a prefab cedar home," he said. "Once I had the foundation in, it took only ten days with a full crew to put the…"

The house was tidy, except for islands of masculine clutter. Surrounding the reclining chair in front of the television were cups, slippers and some half-opened mail. She looked toward the staircase leading to the upper level. "Is your bedroom up there?"

"Let me show you."

Her anticipation grew. *This is it.* They were going to the bedroom.

At the top of the staircase, he pointed to an open door. Heart racing, she entered his office. *What?* Her gaze scanned the huge room with a wall of windows. He pointed out that the view from the window allowed him to look at his chopper, the barn and to see all the way to one of the near meadows where cattle were grazing.

Though she was interested in his livelihood, she hadn't come to his home for a lecture about rescue helicopters and ranching. Striding purposefully, she circled his desk to stand in front of him. *It's now or never.*

She reached up and glided her right hand around his neck. Before she could change her mind, she pressed her mouth against his. For a moment, her pulse stopped. Her lungs ceased to breathe. She existed in limbo, waiting and waiting for his response.

When he pulled her into his arms, excitement gushed through her. She'd never felt so intensely alive. As he deepened the kiss, he pressed hard against her, leaning her back against the desk. She thought he might sweep his arm across the cluttered surface of his desk, shove all his papers onto the floor and make love to her right here. A sexy, dramatic idea, but she wanted to go slower, to savor every caress.

His hand was on her breast, kneading the soft flesh and claiming her as his own. He had taken control of their lovemaking, and she was happy to follow his lead.

Staring down into her eyes, he unbuttoned her muslin blouse. His rough hands pulled the fabric aside. Her breasts pushed against her lacy white bra. Her chest was heaving as she gasped for air.

He stepped back a pace. "My bedroom is down the hall."

"Okay."

Holding her against his chest, he moved toward the door. Though she was walking, her feet seemed six inches off the floor. He nuzzled her ear and whispered, "When you said you wanted to see my house, I was hoping this was what you meant."

"I wasn't exactly being subtle."

On the landing outside the office, he kissed the top of her head. "There's something I've wanted to do from the first minute I saw you."

"What's that?"

He took both of her hands and pulled her into his bedroom. "I want to unfasten your braid."

Still holding his hands, she swung in a circle and sat on his king-size bed. "You have my permission."

He sat behind her and leaned forward to give her a small kiss on the nape of her neck. She arched her back as he tugged at the plaits in her hair.

The quiet made her nervous. She had to say something. "I like your house. Did you decorate yourself?"

"I had help from a girlfriend."

Well, that wasn't what she wanted to hear. She didn't want to think of his house as the cattle-ranch version of a bachelor pad. "Was that the long-distance relationship that went wrong?"

"Nope. It was the lady before her. She kept telling me that I needed my own place, and she was right. Having a separate house helped me have a life that wasn't all about the ranch. Unfortunately, that life didn't include her."

A chunk of her unbound hair fell over her shoulder. "You've had a lot of girlfriends."

"Not really," he said. "What about you? Have there been other men in your life?"

"Of course." She could be vague and push the truth away, but she wanted to explain herself. He needed to know what he was getting into before their lovemaking went any further. He might back off, might be freaked out by her lack of experience. But she had to stick to the truth, even if it meant losing the man she had dreamed about for so many years. "Here's the deal, Aiden. I've never been in love."

With slow strokes, he combed his fingers through her hair. "I'm going to need more explanation."

"That's fair." She wanted to lie back and let nature take its course. "You should know the truth."

From behind, he slipped his arms around her waist, rested his chin on her shoulder and whispered, "You can tell me anything, Tabitha."

The use of her full name seemed special and intimate. Few people even knew that name. "I've never, you know…"

"Tell me."

"I'm still a virgin."

She felt the muscles in his arms clench. Afraid

that he was going to pull away from her, she held herself very still.

"A virgin midwife," he said. "Ironic."

"Yes."

"Is this your way of telling me to back off?"

"No."

"How did this situation come about?"

"A long time ago, I imagined the ideal man. Strong. Handsome. Brave. He was everything I wanted, and no other man could ever measure up to him. I'd be kissing a boyfriend, and the image of my ideal man would come into my head, and I'd know that the boyfriend was nothing but a pale reflection."

"And you wouldn't compromise."

"I can't give myself in halfway portions." She turned around in his arms so that she was facing him. "It's you, Aiden. My ideal man has always been you."

He brushed a light kiss on her lips. "No pressure, huh?"

"Are you up for the challenge, cowboy?"

"You bet."

He stretched her out on his bed and slowly undressed her. As her clothing fell away, so did her inhibitions. She wanted to see his body, wanted to feel him. She peeled off his shirt and frankly stared at the breadth of his chest and the intriguing pattern of chest hair that arrowed down to his belt buckle. He was handsome and virile and everything she imagined.

In a matter of moments, they were wrapped in a naked embrace. Moonlight through the window shone on their legs as they intertwined. His hard arousal pressed against her, and she was amazed by how natural their lovemaking felt—natural and perfect, almost ideal.

Gently but firmly, he caressed her waist and her hips and her inner thighs, until she opened herself to him. She wanted him inside her, had never wanted anything more in her whole life. Their kisses went from sweet to fiery hot. *A virgin midwife.* As he had pointed out, it was ironic.

She was an expert when it came to the female reproductive system, including what happened during sex. In detail, she could have identified her physical reactions complete with hormonal references and a detailed explanation of the interconnected limbic system. But her mind went blank.

She felt good, oh so good, and that was the only information she needed. She reveled in her heightened sensations. Fireworks popped behind her eyelids. Goose bumps marched up and down her naked skin. With every touch, every kiss, every thrust, the intensity accelerated. She didn't think she could go any higher, and then came the explosion of relief. There were no words to describe it.

Completely satisfied, she lay on the bed beside

him. Had this really happened? She was aware that
at some point he'd gotten a condom from the drawer
in the bedside table. For that, she was grateful.

Snuggled against his chest, she exhaled a sigh.
For everything, she was grateful. "Can we do it
again?"

"Was it ideal?"

"I wouldn't change a thing."

He twirled a lock of her hair between his fingers.
"I never knew you had a thing for me, even though
I should have figured it out. You gave me a clue."

"I did?"

He reached over and touched the shamrock pendant she was wearing, the gift he'd given her long
ago. "You weren't saving this necklace because it's
valuable. Your attachment has to be sentimental."

"A lucky four-leaf clover," she said. From now
on, the necklace would represent this—the lucki-
est night of her life.

Chapter Seventeen

The next morning, Aiden slipped out of bed early. Before leaving the bedroom, he made sure Tab was cozy under the covers. It gave him immense satisfaction to tuck the dark brown comforter around her naked body while she slept soundly, breathing steadily through slightly parted lips. When he kissed her forehead, she wriggled and made a soft murmur that reminded him of a purring kitten. He was tempted to wake her and start the day off right by making love again.

But he could wait. He wanted their first morning together to be special, with fresh coffee and a civilized breakfast with normal conversation. For a while, they could forget about investigating. This would be their time.

He pulled on his jeans, left the bedroom and went downstairs to the kitchen. Ideally, he'd put together a tray of food with a napkin and a single red rose in a vase. Ideally?

She'd called him her ideal man, and he wasn't

sure he liked the title. He'd spent much of his life trying to be perfect, taking care of the ranch and making sure everybody else was happy. *Nobody's perfect.* Sooner or later, he'd disappoint her, and he didn't want to see the look in her bright blue eyes when she realized he wasn't ideal, after all.

Barefoot, he padded across the tile floor in the kitchen. He ground the beans and set the coffeemaker to brew. Food supplies in his refrigerator were scant, but he could make do with a couple of eggs, bread and chunk of cheese that hadn't turned green.

A glance at the digital clock told him it was twelve minutes after eight o'clock. Chores on the ranch would be well under way. Breakfast in the main house would be already prepared, which meant he had the option of running over there and grabbing a couple of plates. But he didn't want to see anyone else, didn't want to share this private time with Tab.

His cell phone on the polished granite countertop rang, and he glared at it. When caller ID showed it was the sheriff, Aiden really didn't want to pick up. An early-morning call was sure to be bad news. He answered anyway. "Good morning, Sheriff."

"I shouldn't be making this call," the sheriff said, "but I owe you for your efforts on the investigation. And I'm hoping you can help me with what I have to do this morning."

His sunny vision of a nice breakfast with Tab disappeared behind a cloud of new responsibilities. Things were about to get nasty again. "Tell me."

"We identified the fingerprints that Joseph Lefthand found at Maria Spotted Bear's house. There were a set of prints on the window and on the door leading into the barn."

Those positions fit with the route for the person Aiden had been chasing. "You got those prints yesterday. Why did it take so long to find the match?"

"We weren't looking in the right place. The prints weren't in the criminal database. They matched a set we had taken recently and hadn't fed into the system." He cleared his throat. "They belong to Clinton Brown, Misty's boyfriend."

"Damn." Aiden hadn't seen this coming.

"I'm on my way to your ranch to arrest him. I already stopped at his parents' house, and they said he didn't come home last night. They weren't worried about him being gone because he stays at the bunkhouse at the ranch sometimes."

"I haven't seen him," Aiden said.

"I'm concerned about taking him into custody. He tried to kill Wally. I have to treat Clinton as a dangerous suspect."

"Give me twenty minutes. If he's here, I'll have him ready to go quietly with you."

"I shouldn't do this." The sheriff paused. "But I trust you. Twenty minutes."

Aiden disconnected the call and set the phone down. When he looked up, he saw Tab standing in the doorway. She wore one of his T-shirts that hung almost to her knees. Her long hair—God, he loved that beautiful hair—fell around her shoulders. Her eyes regarded him steadily.

"All I heard was 'fingerprints,'" she said.

"The prints found at your grandma's house belong to Clinton."

She gaped. "I can't believe it. Clinton shot Wally?"

"It seems like that." He glanced longingly at the coffeemaker. "I have twenty minutes to find Clinton and get him ready to turn over to the sheriff."

"I'm coming with you. Don't even think about arguing with me. I'll be ready before you have your boots on."

Regretfully, he watched her pivot and run back through the house toward the staircase. His hope for a sweet, peaceful morning was gone.

AFTER A PHONE CALL to Blake, Aiden learned that Clinton hadn't spent last night in the bunkhouse. He hadn't showed up for work yesterday. His Jeep was nowhere at the ranch. He'd run away, which was absolutely the worst thing he could do. Fleeing was considered the desperate act of a guilty man.

The best way to find Clinton was through Misty. As Aiden hurried toward the main house with Tab at his side, he checked his watch. "I've got eight minutes."

"I still can't believe that Clinton is a killer."

"Look at the facts," he said. "Clinton had access to the gun when David was shot. It's only his word that he was unconscious. Then, he had a fight with Ellen Jessop. Now, his fingerprints are at your grandma's house."

"That's what you call 'circumstantial evidence,' right? Clinton has a knack for being in the wrong place at the wrong time, but that doesn't make him a serial killer."

He sure as hell hoped not. It bothered him that the father of Misty's baby might be capable of such heinous violence. Approaching the front porch, he said, "I'm going to talk to Misty alone. This isn't a time for worrying about her stress level. I need answers about Clinton, and I need them now."

"Should I explain to the others what's going on?"

"That would be wise."

He charged through the front door and went to the kitchen where his mom sat with Maria Spotted Bear. "Where's Misty?"

"Still in bed," his mom said as she rose to her feet. "What's the matter?"

"Tab will explain."

He pivoted and rushed to the staircase. In less than five minutes, the sheriff would be here. Without knocking, Aiden opened the door to Misty's room.

She sat in a pink upholstered chair by the window, fully dressed with her hands resting on her belly. Her eyes were red as though she'd been crying, and her expression was uncharacteristically grave.

"Where's Clinton?"

"I don't know."

"He didn't come to work yesterday. Did he contact you?"

Hesitantly, she said, "I've talked to him. And he sent me text messages."

"If you really want to protect him, you'll tell me where he is. Running away like this makes him look like he's got something to hide."

"He knew what it would look like," she said. "That's why he took off."

"The sheriff is going to be here in a couple of minutes. If you're hiding Clinton, you'll be arrested as an accessory. Misty, you could go to jail. I know you care about Clinton. But he's not worth it."

"You don't understand."

"Fine," he said. "You've got thirty seconds to explain what Clinton was doing at Maria Spotted Bear's house."

"He was playing detective. He thought Wally the Buffalo Man might know something and went looking for him. But Clinton wasn't the only person who was searching for the old man. He saw somebody else."

"Who?"

"A guy in a ski mask. Clinton thought it was Aspen Jim, but he wasn't sure."

"And then?"

"He followed them to Maria Spotted Bear's house. He saw the guy shoot Wally and run away. Clinton tried to use his phone to call 911, but he couldn't get a signal from inside the barn. If you don't believe me, you can ask Tab about that. She's told me that it's hard to get a signal. She said—"

"Stay on track, Misty."

"Okay." She nodded. "I don't want to go to jail."

"I don't want that, either." He leaned over her and patted her hand. "You have to cooperate and tell the truth. Then, it'll all work out okay."

"The truth hasn't worked out for Clinton. He knew it wouldn't."

"He must have seen us arrive in the chopper."

"Right," she said.

"Why didn't he approach us?"

"He was afraid you'd think that he shot Wally. Everything is working against him. He looks guilty. So, he made sure that Tab saw him at the window, and then he ran and led you to the barn where you could help Wally."

The story she told was too stupid to be made up. "I believe you."

"Do you, really?" She looked up at him with wide eyes.

From the moment they found Wally, Aiden had been bothered by the fact that the supposed intruder at Maria Spotted Bear's house had directed them toward the injured man. And Tab had mentioned that someone else used compression on the gunshot wounds. She'd thought it was Wally himself but Clinton might have applied first aid.

He stared hard at his sister. "If you know where Clinton is, you've got to tell."

"I don't know," she said miserably.

"The sheriff is going to start a manhunt. If what Clinton told you is true, the sheriff isn't the only person who wants to find him. The killer will be looking, too."

"You can check the text messages he sent to me. He never says where he is."

Red and blue lights flashed through her window as the sheriff's vehicle pulled up to the house. The sheriff wouldn't want to leave without taking someone into custody. Aiden would have to do some fast talking to keep his sister out of jail.

THE TEXT MESSAGES SAVED Misty...for now. With the sheriff looking over his shoulder, Aiden read the messages on his sister's phone—touching little notes from Clinton, talking about how much he loved her and their baby and apologizing for making mistakes. He never mentioned anything about a location.

Though the sheriff was unconvinced when Misty explained how Clinton happened to be at Maria Spotted Bear's house, he was glad to have another reason to look at Aspen Jim as a suspect. Nobody, except for Woody and Chuck, liked that con man. Maybe this time, Aspen Jim wouldn't have an alibi.

After the sheriff left, Aiden knew they needed to investigate further. Not only did he have to keep Misty out of jail, but he had to clear suspicion from her idiot boyfriend, as well. If Clinton was arrested for these crimes, Misty would be next. She was the Bonnie to his Clyde.

Aiden and Tab were back in the chopper, headed to the hospital in Billings. The only person who could say definitively that Clinton hadn't shot him was Wally, and the old man was close to regaining full consciousness.

As the helicopter swooped through a clear blue sky, Aiden looked over at her. Tab always seemed happy when they were flying. The lady liked to be in the air. He spoke into his headset. "Maybe we can catch dinner at a nice restaurant, someplace with candlelight."

"Don't get your hopes up. If we get any useful information from Wally, we need to act right away."

He agreed. They hadn't told the sheriff that they were going to the hospital, and Aiden was pretty sure that he and Tab were no longer welcome in the police investigation. "We're too close to Clinton. If the sheriff finds out what we're doing, he's not going to be happy."

"Unless the evidence we find makes things worse for him."

"What the hell was Clinton thinking? Running around by himself? Trying to track down clues from Wally?"

"Come on, Aiden." She punched his arm. "Isn't that exactly what we're doing right now?"

"It's different."

"I'm not saying that you have to like Clinton or welcome him into your family with open arms, but he's not a bad guy. He's trying to find the killer."

"And putting himself in danger."

"Again," she said, "isn't that like you?"

Aiden didn't want to admit that he and Misty's boyfriend were similar in any way, shape or form. Still, he knew that Clinton had been trying to do the right thing and marry his sister. And, according to Blake, Clinton was turning out to be a decent ranch hand. And he loved Misty. "Okay. Maybe the kid isn't so bad, after all."

"Probably not a serial killer." She leaned forward for a better look through the windshield and her long ponytail fanned out across her shoulders. "Of all the people we've talked to, there's only one that makes me think he's disturbed enough to be a psycho killer."

"Aspen Jim?" he guessed.

"I could see him committing murder for money, like a hit man. And I wouldn't be surprised if he was a rapist. But I don't think he's the type to abduct women, tie them up and dispose of the bodies on the rez. That takes a certain kind of horrible obsession. It reminds me of Bert Welling and his spotless jumpsuits."

"But Bert has lived in Henley for at least ten years. Why would he start killing now?"

"This might not be the beginning. He might have a tidy stack of rotting corpses buried in his backyard." She cocked her head to one side. Even while talking about dead bodies, she was beautiful. "There's something dark in Bert Welling. My grandma would call it a curse."

"And a profiler would call it obsessive compulsive."

"Different words for the same thing."

They flew over the chiseled rimrock formation toward the skyline of Billings. They couldn't land at the hospital helipad because it needed to be kept clear for emergencies. Instead, he'd leave the helicopter at a local hangar and take one of the rental cars.

Aiden didn't much care for trips into the city, but today the hive of activity beckoned to him. He wanted to share experiences with Tab, to see new places and taste new foods.

"I didn't want to spend the day talking about serial killers," he said. "Not after last night."

"It would have been nice to spend some time alone, just being together." Her eyes flashed. "Maybe making love."

"Definitely making love." He glided his hand down her arm. "This is kind of different for me. I like to take my time when I'm getting to know a lady. Things between us have been moving like lightning."

"Not really. We've known each other for most of our lives. We played together when we were kids. And I spent that summer when I was sixteen with a major crush on you."

"But I haven't known you as a woman."

She leaned forward so she could look him directly in the eye. "I think you like to go slow so you can keep everything under control. Neither of us expected to fall into bed together so quickly. It's a little bit wild."

"More than a little," he agreed.

"It's kind of exciting, isn't it? I'm a practical, responsible person and so are you. I don't get swept away by passion."

"Any regrets?"

"None," she said.

That was good enough for him. Starting today, he'd push his plans and concerns aside. Instead of responsible, he'd be spontaneous, letting life take him to places he'd never been before.

But first, they had to catch a killer.

Chapter Eighteen

Because Wally was under police protection, he had a private room at the end of the hallway on the third floor. Tab was glad to see that the old man was being treated well. As the only witness in a potential serial killer case, the local police ought to be taking real good care of him. The uniformed officer on guard duty outside his room knew her and Aiden from yesterday, and he was obviously happy to see them. The poor guy must be bored to death after sitting for hours in a sterile hospital corridor.

He pumped Aiden's hand. "We've got some new information on the case. The autopsies."

"Great," Aiden said. "What did they show?"

Before speaking, he glanced up and down the hall. The Billings police were being careful not to alert the public to the possibility of a serial killer. They didn't want a panic.

In a low voice, the officer said, "The girl's injuries were consistent with the other victim. We're assuming that they were both killed by the same person."

"Was there any indication that there might have been two killers?"

"Not that I heard about." The officer raised an eyebrow. "Is that one of the theories? Two killers?"

"It's been suggested." Aiden shrugged. "What about David Welling?"

"Shot by a .30 caliber hunting rifle, but you already know that. We've got the murder weapon. Cause of death was internal bleeding. The bullet nicked his heart."

"Anything else?"

"Let me see if I can remember." The officer looked up and to the left. "Three cracked ribs, broken wrist, two broken fingers. Scars on his back and buttocks."

Tab was surprised. "Was he beaten before he was shot?"

"These were all old injuries. Some from childhood. Others when he was a teenager."

"He was abused." Nothing enraged her more than the harming of an innocent child. Bert told them that David's father was an alcoholic, but he hadn't mentioned the abuse. "Are there criminal reports or records about David's injuries?"

The officer shook his head. "None that we could find. David wasn't taken to a hospital for treatment. The poor kid had to heal on his own."

Bert Welling dropped a few notches lower in her estimation. He should have recognized that his nephew was being abused. He should have stopped it. Poor David had led such a terrible, unhappy life. No wonder Misty's casual flirting became so important to him. He must have cherished any hint of love, no matter how small.

Aiden nodded toward the hospital room. "Has Wally been able to answer any questions?"

"He's got answers, but they don't make sense," the officer said. "He just babbles about the moon and monsters with two faces."

"The moon," she said, "that's new. What's he been saying about the moon?"

"I don't know. I just heard moon or moonlight."

"Is it okay for us to talk to him?"

The officer stepped aside. "Knock yourself out."

In the private room, a blonde nurse in blue scrubs checked Wally's vitals. Most people look worse in the hospital, but Wally's appearance was much improved in spite of the IV line, the monitor, the nasal cannula, the dressing that covered his chest wound and the bandage wrapped around his head. The ugly hospital gown was cleaner than anything she'd seen the Buffalo Man wear. His patchy beard was shaved clean.

With his eyes closed, he seemed to be having a pleasant nap. A blanket covered him up to his chest. Though it was only eleven o'clock in the

morning, a tray with a half-eaten lunch was on the
bedside table.

Aiden stood beside his bed. "Are you awake,
Wally?"

The old man twitched his nose but said nothing. Tab was pretty sure that he'd heard Aiden but
didn't want to respond.

"I need to talk to you," Aiden said. "I want to
ask you some important questions."

Wally pried one eyelid open and made a weak
murmur that had Aiden leaning close so he could
hear.

Tab turned to the nurse. Quietly, she said, "That
looks like a lunch tray. Did he have a special order?"

"He wasn't interested in breakfast. He wanted an
egg salad sandwich and ice cream, so that's what I
got him."

"That was nice of you. Out in the real world,
Wally doesn't have anybody to take care of him. I
imagine he's enjoying all this attention."

The nurse cocked a cynical eyebrow. "Some people like being in a hospital."

"How's he doing?"

"Would you like to talk to his doctor?"

"Not necessary." Tab knew that waiting for the
doc could take quite a while. "I'm more interested
in his comfort level. Is he on pain meds?"

"He's pretty well doped up and not coherent."

"The officer said he mentioned the moon."

"Half-moon," she said. "He makes a sweepin[
gesture with his hand and says 'half-moon' as i[
we ought to understand what he means."

"I have a pretty good idea." "Half-moon" had t[
be a reference to the cave. "Thanks."

She took a position next to Aiden at the side o[
Wally's bed. It was better to let him do the talk[
ing because Wally knew him and trusted him. I[
the old man was going to say anything useful, he'[
confide in Aiden.

Straining to hear Wally's mumbling, she presse[
against Aiden. He moved his arm, grazing the sid[
of her breast, and she had to stifle a gasp. Whe[
she was close to him, all her senses sharpened. H[
didn't wear cologne but there was a lingering scen[
of aftershave and another smell that reminded he[
of leather and wind across the prairie.

Making love last night had changed her in way[
she couldn't describe, except to say that she like[
the feeling. She had a new confidence and strength[
an awareness of herself as a woman. And sh[
couldn't wait until they made love again.

If that didn't happen, if he didn't want to be witl[
her, she knew the rejection would hurt. She'd sur[
vive, but the pain of that loss would be so deep tha[
she couldn't stay in this area where she might ru[
into him. She'd run away, go back to Missoula[
find another home, another lifestyle, another life[

Aiden glanced at her and spoke quietly. "I'm no[

getting much from him. The same stuff about monsters in the night."

"Ask him about Half-Moon Cave," she said. "The nurse mentioned it."

"That's a start." He looked toward the hallway. "We ought to get the officer in here. If Wally says anything significant, we need a witness."

She went into the hall and motioned to the officer. "Aiden thinks he's ready to talk."

The officer pulled out a notepad and pen, followed her into the room and stood on the opposite side of the bed. Aiden gave him a nod as he touched Wally's scrawny, pale arm. "What did you see at Half-Moon Cave?"

"It's a bad place. Evil lives there. I heard screaming. Not like when the kids were having parties."

"Did you go closer?"

"The screaming stopped. I figured I was wrong. It was just those kids, those damn kids and their beer parties."

"Did you see them?"

"Two men. They were loud and angry. None of my business. No, sir, I don't go looking for fights."

She imagined Wally in his buffalo robe, hiding behind clumps of sage brush and watching everything. In his way, he'd become a guardian of the reservation land. Nothing happened that he didn't know about.

Aiden asked, "When was this?"

"A week, maybe."

"Is that when you saw the blonde girl? The girl named Ellen?"

"She was loud when she laughed. She made an echo." He opened his eyes wider and blinked. "At Half-Moon Cave, that's when the two-face must have seen me. I ran away, but he sees everything. And he's fast. You can't escape him—no, sir. You can't escape."

His words faded into a mumble, and he closed his eyes. This might be all they got from him, and it wasn't going to help clear Clinton from suspicion.

Aiden switched positions with her. "Talk to him about your grandma's house."

She smiled down at the old man. "Maria Spotted Bear sends her best wishes for your recovery. She's sorry she wasn't home when you came calling."

Without opening his eyes, Wally said, "Kind woman."

"And she makes yummy pies." Appealing to his senses might get him to wake up. "And she grows herbs, fragrant herbs like rosemary and lavender."

His nose twitched and he smiled.

"When you came to visit," Tab said, "the house was dark. Did you go inside?"

He shook his head. "I knew something bad was following me. An evil spirit. Didn't want to bring it inside."

"And you had to hide."

"I went to the barn." His lower lip quivered. "That's where he got me. Two-face attacked me. I told the sheriff. I already told him."

"It's okay," she said in the same soothing voice she used with women in labor. "You don't have to talk about it. I want you to breathe and relax. Let yourself go quiet."

When his agitation had passed, she asked, "After the two-face left you to die, did someone else come to you?"

"A man."

Beside her, she heard Aiden murmur, "Good job, Wally. Tell us about the man."

"I was cold. He covered me with my robe. He tried to help." Wally opened his eyes and looked at her. "Then I saw an angel. That was you."

"What about the man who helped you? Did you know him?"

"He was young. Used his cell phone. Strong hands. I might know him. Don't remember."

She looked across the bed at the officer who was scribbling in his notebook. Wally's information matched the story Misty told them. This might be a break for Clinton.

Leaving Wally to sleep, they went into the hallway. The officer had his cell in hand. "I need to get this information to the chief. Where's this Half-Moon Cave?"

"Not far from where David was shot," Aiden said. "Thanks for letting us see him."

"I should be thanking you. This is a good lead."

Aiden took her elbow and directed her down the hall. He was moving too fast for conversation, and she knew he had a purpose. As soon as they were on the sidewalk outside, he pulled out his cell phone. "I need to make a couple of phone calls."

"Are we going to Half-Moon Cave?" she guessed.

"And taking Sheriff Fielding with us," he said. "I want to get this cleared up as soon as possible."

"I'm kind of surprised that the cave wasn't searched before," she said. "When everyone was looking for Misty's mystery shooter, it seems like the cave would be a good hiding place."

"We checked it out but didn't search thoroughly. The cave is on the other side of the river from where David was killed."

She understood the logic. The Little Big Horn River formed a natural barrier that ran through the rez with very few bridges crossing from one side to the other. Though the current usually rolled lazily along, it was too deep and wide for a vehicle to cross.

While Aiden made his call to the sheriff, she sat on a stone bench under a honey locust tree in a landscaped area outside the hospital. Casting back in her memory, she visualized the place where she'd seen Clinton's Jeep stuck in the almost dried creek bed. The brush at the edge of the river had obscured the view of the water's edge.

On the opposite side, about a hundred yards beyond the riverside cottonwoods and rugged shrubs, a wall of rugged, sandstone cliffs stretched for nearly two miles. Half-Moon Cave looked like a giant hand had reached down and torn a chunk from the wall, leaving a shape that resembled a moon coming halfway over the horizon.

When Tab had been at the Jeep and with Misty, she hadn't been looking toward the cave. The shooter could have fired the rifle, fled into the brush and crossed the river. From there, he could have run or taken a mountain bike to get to the cave or beyond that where David's van must have been parked. When Aiden had searched from the sky, he hadn't gone toward the cave. He'd stayed on the west side of the river.

It was such a simple solution. The shooter had escaped because they were all looking in the wrong direction. The story Misty had told them wasn't a lie. Nor was her unlikely tale of why Clinton's fingerprints were found at Maria Spotted Bear's house.

When Aiden finished his calls, he didn't look happy. He sat on the bench beside her. His shoulders slumped.

"Misty took off," he said.

Chapter Nineteen

After returning to the ranch house, Tab stood at the porch railing and watched as the helicopter rose from behind the barn and swooped toward Henley. Aiden wasn't leaving her behind; they had decided on a divide-and-conquer strategy. While he flew with the sheriff and a couple of deputies to Half-Moon Cave, she would talk to his mother and try to figure out where Misty had gone.

Sylvia stood beside her. In her trembling hand, she held the note that Misty had left behind.

"If I'd known what she was planning," Sylvia said, "I would have lassoed and hog-tied the girl. She told me she was going to the supermarket. Then, I found this."

Tab took the note. Written in purple ink with Misty's flamboyant scrawl, it said: "Don't worry. I'm going to be gone for most of today. Please, Mom, don't worry. I love you."

"When did she leave?" Tab asked.

"A couple of hours ago. She took off a little after

ten o'clock. You and Aiden had just left for Billings. Why would she do this? Is it Clinton? Do you think she's meeting up with Clinton?"

"I don't know what to think."

Tab found it hard to believe that Misty had been planning this escape earlier today. Her attitude had been subdued without a single giggle. She'd looked them straight in the eye and said that she didn't know where Clinton had gone. Getting ready to run away with him? Tab didn't think so. Misty wasn't that good a liar.

Sylvia raised both hands to cover her face. "I feel terrible."

"It's not your fault." Tab wrapped her arm around the other woman's shoulders and led her inside. "Let's put our heads together. We can find her."

"Why doesn't Aiden want to tell the sheriff about Misty?"

"Don't worry." Tab inadvertently echoed the note. "If there's any reason to think she's in danger, we'll organize search parties. But for right now, let's keep the sheriff in the dark. He might think Misty has gone on the run."

"That doesn't make sense. Why would she run?" Sylvia's voice cracked. "She's not guilty."

"Sometimes, innocence isn't enough."

It would kill Sylvia to see her pregnant daughter behind bars. The Gabriels were a proud family.

Suspicion of murder wasn't supposed to happen to people like them.

In the kitchen, her grandma directed them to seats at the table and placed steaming mugs of tea before them. "Chamomile and valerian with a pinch of mint," she said. "This will settle your nerves."

"No offense," Sylvia said, "but it's going to take more than tea to make me feel better."

"We start with a calm spirit—" Maria Spotted Bear offered her wisdom "—then we will reach a good conclusion."

Tab lifted the mug to her nose and took a sniff of the fragrant potion. She used this same formula to help pregnant women who couldn't get to sleep. "Before Misty left, did she do anything unusual?"

"She was on the phone. She's always on the phone."

"Could she have been talking to Clinton?"

"I don't know," Sylvia said miserably. "I don't want to blame him. If anything, Clinton has been a good influence on Misty. He wants to settle down with her, wants to take care of their baby."

Tab had an idea. "When Misty and Clinton wanted to be alone, where did they go?"

"I wish I knew. Misty used to confide in me. We used to have that kind of relationship. I was so proud of her. She got good grades in school, she was a cheerleader and she had friends. She had ambitions. Everybody liked her."

"And then?"

"It started when she got her driver's license. She was never home. She didn't talk to me anymore."

Tab had heard this story many times before. Young women—even more than young men—were given to bouts of foolishness when they reached the age of independence. Misty had taken a leap into Clinton's arms. She'd fallen in love. They'd made a baby.

"Did she mention any special place?" Tab asked. They were both teenagers living with their parents. Making love in their family homes wouldn't have been feasible. "I hate to say this, but there might have been a motel."

"That's real doubtful," Sylvia said. "Everybody in Henley and this area knows our family. Misty wouldn't have taken a chance on getting caught."

Talking to Misty's friends might lead to useful answers, but there wasn't time to break through the teenager code of silence. And Tab didn't want to start the rumor that Misty was gone.

She tried a different tactic. "During the summer I lived here, Misty and I wrote every day in our diaries. Did she keep that up?"

"She did for a long time, but I don't know where she'd keep a diary. I respected her privacy and never had cause to search my daughter's room. She doesn't do drugs or drink too much." Sylvia winced. "At least, I don't think she does."

Tab rose to her feet. "I'm going upstairs to her room to look around."

"Before you leave," her grandma said, "the BIA agent has been trying to reach you."

"Laura Westerfall?"

"She said it was important."

"I'll talk to her later."

"Tabitha," her grandma snapped, "listen to me. Agent Westerfall offered you an opportunity. You must answer her."

Tab had enough on her plate without worrying about setting up a health center that would serve the pregnant women on the rez and in Henley. Initially, the idea appealed to her. That was before she'd made love to Aiden.

If Tab said yes to the project, she'd be committed to staying in the area for an extended period of time, and she wasn't ready to make that decision. The newly formed relationship with Aiden was tentative. If it blew up in her face, she didn't want to be near him.

"I'll talk to Agent Westerfall soon," she promised as she dashed from the kitchen to the staircase.

Standing in the threshold of Misty's room, Tab took a moment to settle her thoughts. Her intense focus on the investigation left little time to consider what was happening in her personal life. She had given her virginity to the man she'd always thought she was meant to be with. Long ago, she'd cast Aiden in the role of soul mate, unbeknownst to him. Making love to him should have meant that her dreams had come true.

But she was young when those dreams were born. She was older now and ought to be wiser. She shouldn't make too much of one night together.

As her gaze circled Misty's room, Tab identified with the odd juxtaposition of a girlish pink velvet chair and a high-tech computer station. On the bedside table, a fluffy stuffed bunny sat beside a book on the stages of pregnancy. The fantasies of a teenager mingled with adult responsibilities and concerns. *Do we ever really grow up?*

She crossed the room and knelt beside the dresser. Misty used to hide her diary in this secret cache under a loose floorboard. When Tab pried it open, she found a small stack of spiral notebooks with years written on them. The last date was four years ago on Misty's thirteenth birthday.

Combing through these pages would have given useful insights into Misty's life, but Tab didn't have hours to pore over these pages, many of which were scribbled pictures of hearts, flowers and whorls. Misty no longer used the notebooks to record her thoughts. Why would she when she had a computer?

Feeling like a voyeur, Tab turned on the laptop. Misty hadn't used password protection, and her documents were readily available. Scanning the labels, Tab smiled in recognition when she read one labeled "D-Abby." When they first started their journals, they joked about writing to Dear Abby with their problems. She clicked on the document and opened the file.

The first entry, the most recent, was dated on the day of the murder. It said: "Nobody believes me. I didn't shoot David. I would never do that. He's been hurt enough."

Tab recalled the autopsy information. The wounds on David Welling's body indicated that he had been abused for a long time. Did Misty know? Or was she referring to a different kind of pain? Either way, her journal hinted that she knew more about David than she'd admitted.

Tab scanned through the entries. Some were only half sentences about a mood or a random thought. Others rambled on and on, especially those about having a baby and how that was scary and happy at the same time.

Tab needed a reference to a place—somewhere Misty might have gone to meet with Clinton. When Tab first got the phone call from Misty, she and Clinton said they were driving around, going off road in his Jeep. At the time, their activity seemed odd. Why would a pregnant woman want to bounce all over the countryside? It seemed more likely that they had simply wanted to be alone. Maybe they'd been on their way to a private hideaway where they could lie in each other's arms and forget about the rest of the world.

Tab did a word search on *Half-Moon* and found a reference from several months ago. Misty had written about an abandoned cabin with a corrugated tin roof that was on the opposite side of the Little Big Horn River and wasn't far from the cave. Not exactly a GPS description, but Tab had something to go on. If she could get Aiden to search with the chopper, they might spot the roof.

With a silent apology to Misty for peeking into her inmost thoughts, Tab closed the Dear Abby journal. In the hallway, she put through a call to Aiden that went straight to voice mail. Cell phone reception—as she well knew—was unreliable on the rez. She'd have a better chance of reaching Aiden if she drove to the cave.

THOUGH AIDEN WASN'T AN authorized lawman, the sheriff hadn't objected when he entered Half-Moon Cave two hours ago with the other searchers. They hadn't known exactly what they were looking for, but evidence hidden in the cave might have been important enough to motivate the nearly fatal attack on the Buffalo Man.

In a dark recess at the back of the cave, one of the deputies had noticed scrapes against the wall and had signaled to the others. A flat piece of wood was held in place by three rocks that leaned at an unusual angle.

"Looks like a door," the sheriff said. "See if you can move those rocks."

"I'll do it." The deputy passed his flashlight to Aiden. "There's not much room here."

Single-handed, he shoved the rocks out of the way, creating other scrapes against the wall. He pried away the board and stepped back. None of them were prepared for what they saw.

The beams from all the searchers' high-power flashlights illuminated a grisly pile of bone and desiccated flesh. Tangles of blond hair clung to a dried skull with the jaw wide open in a silent scream. Another skeleton had knees drawn up to the chin. Rotting ropes fastened wrist bones and ankles, but there were no shreds of clothing or buttons or zippers. The victims had been naked when their remains were discarded in this dark, narrow chamber.

The sheriff squatted down and shone his light on a piece of rope. "This knot is different from the ones used on Ellen Jessop."

"He could have changed his method," a deputy said. "These bodies have been here for a good, long while."

"How many do you think there are?"

"Six or seven, at the least."

"How long?" Aiden asked. "How long have they been buried?"

"I'm no expert on decomposition," the sheriff said, "but this isn't a recent grave. They've been dead for years."

The recent disappearances of young women had opened the door to an extended history of killing. These bones offered mute testimony to a horror that had been too long hidden.

"We need to end this," Aiden said quietly.

"We will." The sheriff rose and took a step back. "Let's go outside. I'll contact the state police and Joseph Lefthand. Identification needs to be done properly."

"Doesn't seem right to leave them here," said the deputy who had discovered the cache of bones in the back wall of the cave when he rolled three heavy rocks out of the way. "I'll stand guard."

"Suit yourself," the sheriff said. "Don't touch anything."

The hiding place was simple but effective. The back wall of the cave was marked by several small openings that led deeper into the earth. Unless you were searching, you'd never notice the rocks that hide the alcove.

Aiden wondered how many people had passed close to this terrible secret and never suspected a thing. People explored this cave all the time. They built campfires near the wide opening at the front.

When he was a teenager, he'd come to parties here. As a kid, he and his buddies played in the cave, using it as a clubhouse. They'd never known. If Wally hadn't remembered screams from this place, the burial chamber might never have been uncovered.

Aiden stepped onto the lip outside the cave and looked downhill to the spot where David Welling was killed. His theory that the shooter had escaped across the river seemed plausible. David's van could have been parked up here. A road came within fifty yards of the cave.

The sheriff joined him. "Finding these bones lets Clinton off the hook for suspicion as a serial killer. He's too young."

"And Wally said he tried to help."

"But I still want to talk to Clinton." The sheriff frowned. "I want to know why he took off running. That's the act of a guilty man."

Aiden kept his mouth shut. No way would he implicate his sister who also appeared to be making a hasty escape. He was anxious to get back to the ranch and see if Tab had made headway on the search for Misty. "Do you need me to fly you back to town?"

"I'll wait for the state police," the sheriff said.

His mood was somber, and Aiden understood his regret and his sorrow. The sheriff and his men had failed to protect these women in life. Now, they felt like they owed these victims. They wouldn't abandon these remains.

"I'm taking off," Aiden said. "If there's any way I can help, let me know."

"I'll be in touch."

He hiked away from the cave. Though the afternoon sun beamed overhead, the sight of those bones cast a dark, angry haze over his vision. Nothing seemed clear. In a world where such senseless, depraved wrongs could be committed, how could anything be right? How the hell could a human being commit those crimes?

The killer had been operating for years. That meant he lived in the area. He was a person they all knew. Aiden might have sat beside him in the diner, might have spoken to him or hired him for seasonal work. He might have shaken the hand that had killed those women.

As he neared the road and the place where he'd left the chopper, he saw another vehicle approaching. It was Tab's van, moving fast enough to kick up a tail of dust.

She parked and hopped out. "Don't you ever check your cell phone for messages?"

"I've been busy."

Coming closer, her expression changed. "What's wrong?"

He didn't want to tell her, didn't want to poison her mind. He only wanted good things for Tab.

Their relationship should be about hope and light and everything that was positive. But he couldn't hide his feelings from her.

She looked at him, and she knew.

Without saying a word, she slipped her arms around him and rested her head on his shoulder. He didn't need comforting, but he welcomed her embrace and held her tightly against him. Her heart echoed his. They were in sync, connected.

"You found a body," she guessed, "hidden in the cave."

"More than one." He inhaled the fresh, sweet fragrance of her hair. "There's not much left of them but bones, old bones."

She shuddered against him. "These killings have been going on for a long time."

A brisk wind swirled around them. Tonight would be colder. He and Tab could sit together in front of the fireplace and find ways to keep each other warm.

"Did Misty come back?" he asked.

"Not yet, but I think I know where she is. We need to take the chopper."

As far as Aiden was concerned, his part in the investigation was over. There should be enough forensic evidence from the remains in the cave to identify

he killer. After that, it was the sheriff's problem
o track down and arrest this monster.

Aiden's only concern was to gather his family
close and make sure they were all safe.

Chapter Twenty

In the chopper, Aiden and Tab hovered in the skies over the Little Big Horn and Half-Moon Cave. During the past few days, his six-passenger Bell Long Ranger had been getting a lot of use, and he was glad he'd taken the opportunity while they were in Billings to refuel. "What happened when you tried calling Misty?"

"I called, texted and sent mental messages," Tab said. "I've gotten no answer. The same is true for Clinton. I sent him a text telling him that he was in the clear and it was safe for him to come back."

"And he didn't reply."

"Not yet." She glared at the cell phone in her hand as though willing it to ring.

"You seem sure that Misty took off to join Clinton."

"It's possible that she heard about a really great shoe sale in Billings and took off," Tab said with a smirk. "Of course, she's running off to see Clinton."

"Not that I could ever understand the way my sister's mind works, I still have to ask. Why?"

"It's a woman thing," she explained. "No matter how many dumb things our men do, we keep thinking we can fix them."

He exhaled a sigh. "Let's find Romeo and Juliet before they get into any more trouble."

"We should go east," she said, "away from the river and the cave. When Misty and Clinton got stuck on the other side of the river, I think they were headed to their hideout."

"First, we scan in the west."

He wasn't going to make the mistake of not covering the whole area. Not again. If he'd circled back around the cave when he first responded to Tab's call, he might have spotted David's van.

"You're the expert," she said.

Aerial surveillance wasn't as accurate as many people assumed. The view of the earth below was expansive, but picking out details was hit or miss unless the searchers were gifted with the vision of a hawk or an eagle.

"We should be able to see a house," he said. "With a corrugated tin roof?"

"According to Misty's description, the roof is rusty, the walls weathered and the windows broken out. The metal cistern beside the house is still operable, but I wouldn't drink any of that water."

"And she wrote about this place in her journal?"

"In great detail," Tab said. "I feel terrible abou prying. When I was looking for clues, I tried not t read her private thoughts, but I couldn't help see ing a few things. She's truly excited about havin the baby, and she loves Clinton."

"Even though she won't marry him?"

"Love doesn't always end in a commitment."

The steady tone of her voice made him think tha she might be talking about herself as well as Misty The idea of marrying Tab hadn't become part of hi thinking, not yet anyway. They'd just taken thei friendship to the next natural level, and he wante a chance to enjoy getting to know her.

"My sister," he said, "has never been big on re sponsibility."

"Not like you."

She shot him a grin. As always, when the were airborne, her mood seemed brighter and les guarded. He could barely take his eyes off her, eve though he was supposed to be staring down at th ground.

"You're no slouch when it comes to being re sponsible," he said.

"When I make a commitment, I carry through. Her blue eyes gleamed as she looked toward him "I had a call from the BIA agent who thinks sh can get funding for a women's clinic."

"I like the idea." If Tab was running a clinic

he'd stay in the area. "There's a need for something like that in this area."

"Pregnant women in cities have more options," he agreed. "There are a lot of obstacles on the rez and in Henley. Not only do these women have to travel great distances to seek medical care, but they often can't afford to deliver their babies in hospitals. And they don't think about prenatal vitamins, postnatal care for themselves or breast feeding. There's most definitely a need, but—" she turned her head and looked out the window again "—I don't know if I'm the right person to do this."

He slowed the chopper to hover. "I want you to stay."

She pointed to the ground. "Over there."

Beside a rocky area with a couple of trees was a tumbled-down shack. He lowered their altitude for a better look. Abandoned dwellings weren't unusual in this area, especially not on the rez where property ownership was more clearly defined by who was taking care of the land than by a deed or contract.

Tab peered through the windshield. "It's not that one. Half the roof is caved in."

She hadn't answered his comment about wanting her to stay, and he decided not to push. Later, there would be time for him to show her how much he wanted her in his life.

In a roughly defined grid, he searched a ten-

square-mile area. The packed earth roads on thi
side of the river were more clearly defined thoug
not well maintained. Nobody was supposed to b
living here, and nobody bothered to keep the ac
cess clear. After they passed another disintegratin
house where only the rock chimney was stand
ing, he returned to the cave. A vehicle belongin
to the tribal police was parked beside Tab's var
Joseph Lefthand stood outside the cave, talking t
the sheriff.

"I hope they've got enough to catch this killer,
he muttered. "God only knows how many live
he's destroyed."

In addition to the women he'd killed, he'd ruine
the lives of their families and friends. Aide
couldn't imagine the emotional pain if Misty ha
been abducted and brutally murdered. When he'
heard that the killer preferred blonde women, he'
been afraid for his sister.

On the west side of the river, he once again lai
out a mental grid, starting at a rise in the prairi
where jagged cliffs blended into forest. From thi
distance, Half-Moon Cave was barely visible. A
graded gravel road made a zigzag through the pine
and evergreens. They quickly noticed four or fiv
cabins that were occupied with wisps of smoke ris
ing from the chimneys.

"They could be staying with someone else,'
he said.

"Misty never mentioned anyone else in her journal. This was her special place to be with Clinton—their private hideaway."

Adjusting the chopper's altitude, they ascended for a more panoramic view. The landscape lay below them like a relief map. "Look for other smoke trails," he said. "It's plenty cold enough for fire."

"That way." She pointed. "I don't see smoke, but there's something shiny. Maybe the tin roof."

In less than a minute, the chopper hovered above a stand of trees that surrounded a very small cabin. It couldn't have been more than two rooms. A metal cistern clung to one side. Parked in the back and covered with branches was Misty's SUV.

"We're here," he said.

"I'm getting a text message." Tab held up her phone. "It says for us to come on in."

"If I wasn't so relieved, I'd kick my sister's tail. She puts us through all this worry, and then acts like she's inviting us for a tea party."

As soon as they landed and the rotors stilled, he heard a sharp cry followed by a moan. He reached into the back of the chopper for his rifle.

"You probably won't be needing your gun," Tab said.

"Didn't you hear the scream?"

"I'm guessing it's Misty. And she's in labor."

He froze with the rifle in his hand. His mind be-

came a static wall of sheer panic. It was time. Hi
baby sister was having a baby.

WISHING THAT SHE'D BROUGHT her midwife gear fror
the van, Tab dashed toward the small cabin an
yanked open the door. She saw Misty lying on
ramshackle bed covered by a surprisingly clea
quilt that she must have brought with her. Her fac
was red, and she was breathing hard at the end c
a contraction.

As soon as Misty saw her, she struggled to s
up. "Don't come in here."

"It's okay," Tab said as she went toward the bec
"You're going to be all right."

Aiden charged into the small room. Trippin
over his own boots, he lurched toward the bed an
leaned across Tab to touch his sister's arm, nearl
smothering them both in the process. "Misty, tel
me you're okay."

"Oh God, Aiden. I'm sorry. I'm so sorry."

The door slammed behind them. A cold voic
said, "She'll be just fine as long as you do what
say."

Tab looked over her shoulder. She was starin;
down the barrel of an automatic pistol. In the dir
light from two windows that had been covered witl
plastic, she saw the gleam of sun-bleached hair
Aspen Jim moved away from the door where he'

een hiding and carefully put distance between
imself and Aiden.

"Drop the rifle," Jim said. "Do it now or I'll
hoot out your sister's knee. She's been bugging the
ell out of me with her moans and groans."

Aiden set the rifle on the floor by his feet.

"Kick it over here," Jim ordered.

"There's no reason to hurt anybody," Aiden said
s he pushed the rifle with his boot. "I need to take
ay sister to the hospital. You can have her SUV."

"Then what? I'd get about two miles away be-
ore you called in the law. No deal." He squatted,
icked up the rifle and stood it in a corner of the
oom. "Don't try anything cute. Even if I'm not a
aarksman, I can't miss at this range."

Tab sat on the bed beside Misty and held her.
obbing loudly, Misty leaned against her. "I thought
was helping Clinton."

"Get her to shut up," Aspen Jim growled. "I can't
tand the noise."

"Misty, look at me." Tab spoke quietly and held
Iisty so she had to look into her face. "You're
oing to be all right. Now, I want you to take a
eep breath."

Misty shook her head. Her cheeks were wet with
ears. "I never should have come here, should have
nown better. He sent me a text. Said I could help
linton. He lied."

Luring Misty to this place had been as simple

as getting a puppy to fetch a tennis ball. But no wasn't the time for recriminations.

"Deep breath," Tab said. "Come on, now. Do i Breathe."

Her shoulders trembled violently as she inhale

"Good. Do it again."

After another breath, Misty was beginning t calm down. At least, she wasn't hyperventilating

Standing beside her, Aiden straightened hi shoulders and spoke to Jim. "What do you want?

"You're going to take me for a ride in that shin chopper of yours, and I'm going to get as far awa from this godforsaken country as I can."

"You can't run far enough," Aiden said. "You' be smart to cooperate, turn yourself in and—"

"Shut up," he yelled. Agitated, he paced forwar and back. "A guy like me can always start over. I'r a cat. I land on my feet."

"Don't run. I'll help you with the cops."

"I said shut up." He leveled his gun at the cente of Aiden's chest. "I'm not taking the rap for this. know what they found in that cave. He showed me.

Though concentrating on Misty, Tab couldn help listening. Aspen Jim was saying that he didn kill the women they found in the cave. Right now she couldn't think of a single reason why he'd li about his guilt or innocence.

"You're not the serial killer," Aiden said. "Thos were old bones, and you've only lived in this are

or a couple of months. The sheriff doesn't sus-
ect you."

"Why should I believe you?"

"The state police and forensic teams are on their
ay right now. They'll prove that those remains are
om years ago." Aiden's voice sounded completely
ational. "Why don't you tell me who showed you
ose bodies? The sheriff will arrest him, and you'll
e free and clear."

Tab felt Misty's body beginning to tense. An-
ther contraction was coming. She wished that
he'd checked the time between this one and the
ist. It was ten minutes, maybe more. Misty was
till in the early phase of labor.

"Here we go," Tab said. "This time, I want you to
oncentrate on your breathing. You said you went to
pregnancy class, right? They talked about breath-
g."

"I don't remember." Misty grasped her hand and
ripped hard. "I can't think."

"Not again." Aspen Jim started his pacing again.
I don't want to hear the moaning. Make her stop."

"That's not going to happen," Tab said. "This
aby is coming whether you like it or not."

"I don't like it," he snapped.

"And I hate you," Misty yelled at him. "You're
ever going to get away free and clear. You're
oing to jail because you're a murderer. You killed
David."

Tab had been focused on the serial killer; sh
hadn't expected this new revelation. Without think
ing, she asked, "Did you see him? Did you see Jin
fire the rifle?"

Glaring at him, Misty said, "Damn right, I did.

"You didn't," Aspen Jim said. "I got away to
fast. You couldn't have seen me."

"Gotcha," Misty said.

Jim winced and shook his head. "Damn."

"Good job," Aiden said to his sister. "Tha
sounded like a confession to me."

"Cut me some slack," Jim said. "I had to do it. I
I hadn't shot David, my partner would have kille
me."

"Why did he want David dead?" Aiden asked.

"The little dipstick got scared. He wasn't totall
innocent, you know. He had a damn good idea wha
my partner was doing, and it didn't bother hin
much until he thought Misty might be in danger
David followed the Jeep out of town to warn her
He was going to betray my partner and me."

"And you couldn't let that happen."

"I didn't kill those girls." Aspen Jim was trem
bling. "I'm not going to jail for something I didn'
do."

"What about the Buffalo Man?" Aiden asked
"Were you the two-face monster that went afte
him?"

"That crazy old coot deserved to be put out of s misery."

"But Clinton saved him."

Misty reacted to her boyfriend's name. "Clinton? id you hurt him, too?"

"He came looking for me, but I got away. Hitched ride out of town and rode the mountain bike here."

Misty let out a fierce groan, and Tab coached er through the pain. This was going to be a dif-cult labor.

Chapter Twenty-One

Strapped into the pilot's seat, there was nothin
Aiden could do about what was happening in th
rear of the chopper where Aspen Jim held his gu
on Misty and Tab. The women had constructed
sort of nest for Misty using the quilt from the cabi
and emergency supplies on board. Given that Mist
was in labor, she seemed to be fairly comfortabl
Her contractions were coming more frequently.

But Aiden really couldn't see what was going o
behind his back. Nor could he hear over the *thwap
thwap* of the rotors and the loud hum of the engin
Aspen Jim refused to let them use the headset in
tercom that made normal conversation possible an
blanked out the noise.

By taking away the headsets, Jim figured he'
eliminate any possibility of calling for help; the
wouldn't be able to communicate with Air Traf
fic Control. He'd also destroyed their cell phones
Aiden's only chance for an SOS was to open th

ine on the communication panel and broadcast the
mbient noise in the chopper. A long shot, at best.

The direction they were headed—south toward
he Big Horn Mountains—was sparsely populated
nd regular ATC surveillance was limited to the
ew regional airports. Aiden's only hope for sum-
noning help was that somebody at an airstrip happened to be randomly monitoring communications
nd got the message.

When Misty let out another wail, Aiden craned
is neck to look over his shoulder. He hated that
is sister was in pain. Again, there was nothing he
could do. The baby was coming. Thank God Tab
vas here.

Thus far, she'd been rock steady. Only once had
er fear surfaced. When they were boarding the
helicopter, she'd gotten close enough to grasp his
and. He'd felt the tremble in her touch, and it made
im angry. He needed all his self-restraint to keep
imself from lashing out at Aspen Jim. He couldn't
isk a fight. Not while Jim had the gun.

He had tried to reassure her. "I'll get us out of
his."

"We'll do it together. You and me."

"That's what I meant."

"But not what you said."

Damn, she was stubborn. Even now, when he
could see the panic shimmering in her blue eyes,
she wouldn't let him shoulder all the responsibil-

ity. This was *their* problem. Together, they woul
fight it.

Being together, it sounded right. He wanted t
be with her in every way. Not just making love, al
though he treasured those sweet, intimate moment
with her above all else. He wanted to go riding wit
her, to wake up beside her in the morning, to watc
the sunset from the porch of his cabin.

They'd get through this. They had to. No weak
willed murderer like Aspen Jim was going to de
stroy his chance at true happiness with Tab.

Through the front window of the chopper, th
snowy peaks of the Big Horn Mountains came
clearly into view. There wasn't much time for Aide
to make his move. Though Jim hadn't stated a spe
cific destination, Aiden was pretty sure he wouldn'
like what he found when they were on the ground
He wanted to gain control of the situation before
they landed.

Jim still hadn't given up the name of his part
ner—the serial killer who had been operating ir
Henley and on the rez area for years. It was clea
that Aspen Jim feared this man and was desper
ate to do his bidding—so desperate that he'd be
trayed his natural con man leanings and become
a killer. Murder didn't come easily to Aspen Jim
His planning was overcomplicated with a bizarre
element of showmanship, similar to his idea of

iver rafting company that included actors on the
anks of the river.

He'd admitted that luring Misty to the hideaway
ad been the first step in his escape. Getting ac-
ess to the chopper had been his real goal, and he'd
nown Aiden would respond to a hostage situation
nvolving his sister.

At Maria Spotted Bear's house, Jim could have
hot poor old Wally and left the body to be found.
nstead, he'd chased the old man and pretended to
e a two-face monster.

When Aspen Jim shot David, he'd managed to
ull off a mysterious escape by swimming the river,
iding a mountain bike and fleeing back toward
own. One complication had led to another and an-
ther. He should have gotten away with it.

But Jim had made a mistake. That error told
Aiden the identity of Jim's so-called partner. He'd
sed Bert Welling as his alibi, and Bert had backed
im up.

Bert had lied. Why? Bert had to keep his own
ecrets, to hide a lifetime of cruelty. Aiden remem-
ered the autopsy report that indicated signs of
buse on David's body. They'd assumed his father
ad hurt the boy, but it was more likely his uncle.
Bert Welling enjoyed inflicting pain on others, es-
ecially young women.

As soon as Aiden had sorted out the logic, he
hought it was obvious that two killers had been

involved. The handsome, sun-bleached blond Jir
had attracted the women. Bert had killed them
Their problem came when Bert escalated his time
table and grabbed too many victims. The disap
pearances attracted attention. His reign of cruelt
would soon be over.

Aspen Jim lurched forward and grabbed ont
the copilot's seat. "I have instructions." He had t
yell over the whirr of the rotors. "Go to Jackrabb
Lake. To the campground."

Though Aiden knew the location, he didn't adm
it. "I don't know where it is. I need to turn on th
GPS for directions."

"So you can call your cop buddies? No way
You'll figure it out."

They were already over the foothills. The land
scape transformed from rolling hills to jagged gran
ite formations and forests of lodgepole pine, fir an
aspen. A light dusting of snow covered the ground
At this time of year, there were no rangers poste
in the National Forest. Officially, the campground
were closed.

Hoping to buy time, Aiden said, "I'm runnin
low on fuel. I might have to land before we get t
the lake."

"Show me the gauge."

Aspen Jim leaned forward to see the instrumen
panel. If he moved a little closer, just six inche
closer, Aiden could reach back and grab the gun

He subtly unfastened his seat belt as he pointed to the fuel gauge. "It's right here."

"You've got a quarter of a tank."

"This isn't like a car. I'm running low." A blatant lie—the chopper could cover another seventy-five to a hundred miles on the fuel he had left.

"You'll make it. You don't want anything to happen to the precious cargo you're carrying in the back of this chopper. Your sister and your girlfriend? You'd better fly right."

Adrenaline rushed through Aiden's veins, urging him to take action. He had to be careful, couldn't lose control. "Are we meeting up with your partner?"

"That's right."

Bad news. The way Aiden figured, Aspen Jim might be convinced not to kill them all. The same wasn't true for Bert Welling. He'd take pleasure in watching them die.

"Hey," Jim pointed with the barrel of his gun. "What's that red light?"

"Nothing important."

"The panel says intercom. That's a communication device." His shout got louder. "You're calling for help."

"I can't talk to anybody without the headset."

"We'll see about that."

He pointed the nose of his gun at the control panel as though preparing to shoot. What the hell?

Was he crazy enough to fire a bullet into the instruments? There wasn't time to argue with Asper Jim. He had to be stopped.

Bolting from the pilot's seat, Aiden flung out his arm, making a frantic grab for the weapon. He almost had it. The gun was mere inches from his grasp.

Jim reacted with a yelp. He yanked his arm backwards and fired a bullet straight up, through the ceiling. The gunshot reverberated inside the plane.

Though Jim pointed the gun at his chest, Aiden couldn't stop now. He had only seconds to take control. It was now or never. He lunged.

In a panic, Jim pulled the trigger. The bullet missed Aiden and went into the cockpit. A burst of sparks exploded from the instrument panel. The chopper swerved wildly.

If Aiden didn't get back to the controls, they would surely crash. He wheeled around on his opponent. He couldn't balance, couldn't get his feet under him. Finally, Aiden landed a heavy blow to Jim's chin. His head snapped back. His knees folded under him.

Tab scrambled from the back, picked up the gun and aimed it at Jim. "The controls," she yelled. "Aiden, get us down."

In an instant, he was back in the pilot's seat. He knew the procedure for emergency landing, but he'd never had to do anything like this before. Jug

ling the directional stick, regaining equilibrium
and decelerating simultaneously, he scanned the
ground below, looking for a safe place to put down
amid rock formations and forest. He'd lost control
of the rudder. The rotors sputtered. They were coming down fast.

With a heavy thud, the chopper hit the ground.

A spark danced across the panel and ignited into
a flame.

If the chopper had been carrying a full tank of
fuel, they might have already exploded. Disaster
was imminent. Aiden had to get Tab and Misty to
safety.

He scooped his sister into his arms and carried
her uphill. His feet slipped in the thin coating of
snow. Tab came behind him. Her arms were full
of blankets and supplies. She still held the gun in
her hand.

A safe distance away from the chopper, he
ducked behind a rock formation and lowered Misty
to the ground. She clung to his neck and gave him
a weak smile. "You're a superhero."

"About time you realized that."

"I've always known. My big brother can do anything."

Tab dropped her load of supplies and knelt beside
them. "You scared me, Aiden. For a minute there,
I didn't think we were going to make it."

"I'd never let anything happen to you."

He touched her shoulder and squeezed lightly. Her face was the most beautiful sight he'd ever seen. Her eyes glowed like blue stars. Her lips were soft and full. He leaned forward to give her a quick peck on the cheek. Instead, he kissed her mouth, and he didn't want to stop.

"Hey," his sister interrupted. "I'm having a baby here."

Pushing himself to his feet, Aiden turned toward the chopper. "I'll be right back."

Before he'd gone five paces, Tab was in front of him, blocking his way. "What are you doing?" she demanded.

"Going back for Jim." The spark on the instrument panel had grown into a cockpit fire. He could see the orange-red flames through the windows.

"You can't risk your life to save his."

"It's wrong to leave him." Aiden's motives weren't altogether noble. "And he has the only cell phone."

He heard yelling from the chopper. Aspen Jim had recovered enough to take action for himself. He stood in the doorway, weaving unsteadily—a terrible and dramatic pose. He flung curses at them, swore revenge.

He paused as though he knew what was coming.

The chopper exploded in a fireball, throwing the rotors, the plexiglass windows and jagged pieces from the body and tail into the sky. A wave of

eat washed over them, pushing them back. Black
.moke darkened the sky. A metallic stench poi-
:oned the air.

Tab looked up at him. "That could have been
·ou."

He folded her into his embrace. Her slender body
molded against him. Though they had spent only
·ne night together, her curves felt familiar and, at
he same time, exciting. They were made to be to-
;ether.

He nestled her close and whispered in her ear. "I
1ever want to be apart from you again."

"We're lucky there's snow on the ground. The
·xplosion shouldn't turn into a forest fire."

"Yeah, lucky."

She tilted her head to look up at him. "I'm sorry
1bout your helicopter."

"I can always get another. The important thing
s that we're safe."

"For how long?"

He knew she was talking about Jim's partner.
They were close enough to Jackrabbit Lake that
3ert would see the flames from the explosion, and
t was entirely possible that he'd come after them.
3ert was a tidy man. He wouldn't like to leave
oose ends.

Chapter Twenty-Two

Tab's first concern was making Misty comfort able. After a rapid search of the mountain terrain they decided on a site beside a tall hunk of granite where they could build a fire. Keeping warm would be an issue tonight.

Working together, she and Aiden built a shelter of branches. Her hands were cold. She hadn't needed gloves at a lower elevation, but now she wished she had them. Her only tool was the pocket knife she carried in her purse. Still, the shelter came together quickly.

Watching them, Misty commented, "I'm impressed, Tab. How did you learn how to do this?"

"My grandma showed me how to build my own sweat lodge. If we had more time, I'd make this into a cozy little house where we could live."

"How much time do we have?" Misty asked. Her casual tone didn't completely mask her nervousness. "My contractions are coming every five minutes."

"I'd like to give you a precise arrival time, but I
n't. First babies are unpredictable."

"Do you think the baby is all right? It's kind of
emature."

Tab left Aiden to handle the building while she
ent to his sister and held her hand. "You're only
few weeks short of full term. There's nothing to
orry about."

Looking up, Misty scanned the skies. The sun
d begun to set, and the clouds were tinted with
agenta and gold. "A rescue team ought to be look-
g for us. That was a giant explosion."

Tab hoped she was right. The flames had already
ied, but a funnel of black smoke rose in the air.
omebody ought to be searching; there had to be
eople who lived in this area. If park rangers had
en on duty, they would have already responded.

Using the quilt and other blankets she'd grabbed
om the chopper, Tab covered the floor inside their
akeshift shelter. When Misty was settled inside,
nother contraction hit. The pain had to be more
ntense than earlier, but Misty had learned how to
reathe and to focus.

"You're doing well," Tab said, "really well."

"I know." Misty licked her lips and forced a
nile. "It's because you're a good teacher."

"You're doing all the heavy lifting. Stay strong."
oosting her confidence was important. "I'm going

to step outside. There's something I have to do wi
Aiden."

"More kissing?"

"Maybe."

The kissing was great, but she really wanted
hear Aiden's conclusions about the serial kille
Not an appropriate conversation to have in fro
of Misty. She needed to concentrate on having h
baby without hearing gory details.

Outside the shelter, she saw Aiden leanin
against a tree trunk. In the explosion, he'd lo
his hat, and he had the collar on his denim jack
turned up. She swung into his arms. "Tell me wh
you figured out. Make it fast. And make it quiet

He murmured, "I can think of something els
that would be fast and quiet."

Though the low rumble of his voice got her er
gine revving, she said, "I want to know what yo
know."

In a whisper, he sketched the broad picture o
two killers with different styles—Aspen Jim an
his partner. "Bert," he said, "is the killer."

An image of the gas station owner popped int
her mind. His gray jumpsuit looked like it had bee
laundered by a dry cleaner. His thinning hair wa
neatly combed. And his hands...his hands wer
spotless. She shuddered. "I knew there was some
thing suspicious about him."

"Most people wouldn't. He's lived in Henley fo

ears and knows everybody. We saw him at Con-
e's house with a baby gift."

She thought of all the young men who worked
r him and came under his dark influence. They
ouldn't have known the terrible things that Bert
ad done. "It took another psychopath like Aspen
m to finally become his partner."

"We were supposed to meet Bert at Jackrabbit
ake," Aiden said. "He might come after us."

"Could be watching us right now."

Misty called out from the shelter. "Tab, I need
ou."

She forced herself to step away from Aiden.
Leave the gun here with me. There's a collaps-
le plastic container for water."

"I know," he said, "it's my container, part of my
mergency supplies. It holds two and a half gal-
ons."

"Find a creek and fill it. I only have one bottle
f water. We're going to need more."

He pressed Aspen Jim's weapon into her hand.
Be careful."

"Back at you."

Inside their shelter, there was only room for Tab
nd Misty. After the contraction passed, she fig-
red it was time to prepare for the next phase in
elivering this baby. "Let's see how far along you
eally are. Take off your clothes from the waist
own. Leave your socks."

"When you were babysitting me, did you eve think we'd end up like this?"

Delivering a baby while being stalked by a se rial killer? Tab could honestly say that scenari had never occurred to her. "I knew we'd alway be friends."

"Really?" Misty brightened.

"Not the kind of friends who talk every day c send messages on the internet. We have a bond you and me. No matter where we are or what we'r doing, we'll always be close."

"Is that what you have with my brother?"

"We're bonding, that's for sure." And she had good feeling about what might come next…if the survived this night.

When Misty was undressed, Tab examined he Without her instruments, she couldn't state he findings in centimeters, but experience told her the Misty was fully effaced and further along in th birthing process than she'd thought.

She pulled a blanket over Misty's bare legs. "Ar you warm enough?"

"Is it possible to be hot and cold at the sam time?"

Misty giggled, and Tab was glad to hear th sound. It meant her spirits were good. "You're al most ready to have this baby. Very soon, you'r going to have the urge to push."

"How will I know when that is?"

"You'll know," Tab said. "And here's what you do. Try to hold back until I tell you it's time."

She had barely finished talking when the next contraction tensed Misty's muscles. In spite of her focused breathing, Misty gave a loud yelp.

During labor, Tab encouraged the mothers to do whatever felt natural. To get into whatever position felt right and to scream if they felt like it. The sound Misty made would lead Bert to them, but they didn't really have anywhere to hide safely from him.

After twenty minutes, Misty was nearly ready to push. Where was Aiden? It shouldn't have taken him this long. Tab tried not to think of the terrible things that might happen. The gun lay on the ground beside her. If she saw Bert, she'd shoot first and ask questions later.

Aiden poked his head into the shelter. "Do you want the good news or the bad?"

"Just talk," Misty snapped. "Don't be cute."

"I've heard about this phase of labor," he said. "It sounds homicidal."

"Your news?" Tab prompted.

"I got water." He plopped the container into the shelter.

"That's good."

"There's no way I'm going to be able to build a fire. The wood is too damp. That's bad. But here comes the really good news."

In the dim light of dusk, she could barely see his grin. Drily, she said, "Knock us out."

He flashed a cell phone. "It's Aspen Jim's. I found it near the wreckage, and I put through a call. A rescue team is on the way."

"Great news," Tab said. But she doubted the rescuers would get here before the baby arrived.

The next contraction was powerful. Misty tried to breathe through it but gave up. "I've got to push. Now. I have to."

Operating more by touch than sight, Tab knew the baby was in position. "Next time," she said, "push for all you're worth."

She noticed that Aiden had left the shelter and had taken the gun with him. He was standing guard, and that gave her a huge measure of relief as Misty went into the last phase of labor.

The head crowned. With Tab offering calm encouragement, Misty pushed with every fiber of her strength. The baby was coming. No stopping it now. A miracle was on the way.

The head was out, then the shoulders and the torso. A fully formed baby boy slipped into Tab's waiting hands. He was a good, healthy size, at least six pounds.

Misty gasped. "Is the baby all right?"

The tiny mouth pursed, and the infant let out a yell.

"He's perfect," Tab said. She swabbed away the

mucus and placed the baby, with the umbilical cord still attached, on his mother's chest.

Aiden looked in. His head was close to Tab's, and she could see the wonder in his eyes.

"You did it," he said to his sister. "I'm proud of you."

"And your nephew," she said with a giggle. "I'm going to name him after Dad. Matthew Gabriel."

He slipped his arm around Tab's waist. "Thank you."

"Misty did all the work."

"You're brilliant, Tabitha. I admire you."

His praise delighted her, and she would have liked nothing more than to sit back and let him tell her over and over that she was terrific. But there were other things to do before the rescue team arrived.

OUTSIDE THE SHELTER, Aiden took a position higher on the hill to watch over his girls and the new infant. Powerful emotions churned inside him. He was ready for a baby of his own, ready to settle down, ready to start the next part of his life. And he wanted to share that life with his beautiful Tabitha.

He didn't usually make huge decisions so quickly, but he'd never been more certain of anything in his life. She was the right woman for him.

He'd put through another call to the rescue team. They'd seen the plume of smoke and knew the location. They needed a chopper. Since Aiden was out of commission, the closest other rescue service was a good forty minutes away. He checked his wristwatch. Less than fifteen minutes were left. Everything had turned out right.

He heard movement behind him and ducked just in time to avoid the knife that slashed through the air. Pivoting, Aiden faced off with Bert Welling. In one gloved hand, he held a knife. In the other, a pistol.

Aiden couldn't believe he'd let down his guard. His own gun was tucked into the waistband of his jeans, accessible but not in his hand.

"Answer one question for me," Aiden said. "What made you hook up with a fool like Aspen Jim?"

"The ladies liked him. They trotted along with him like lambs to the slaughter."

Hoping to buy time, Aiden kept talking. "Did you ever use a different partner? Maybe David?"

"That boy was worthless. After everything I did for him, he was fixing to betray me. Over what? He thought Misty gave a damn about him. The boy was too dumb to live."

"You know, Bert, if you leave right now, I won't tell anybody you were here."

"How about this, Aiden. First, I'm going to kill you. Next, I'll slice up that pretty Crow girl you've been hanging around with. She'll be my main course. For dessert, I'll kill Misty and her bastard."

In the moonlight, Aiden saw Bert's lip curl into a grin of pure evil. He was enjoying his fantasy. It would be the last thought he ever had.

Diving to the right, Aiden pulled his gun. As soon as he hit the ground, he fired. Not fast enough. Bert had gotten off two shots of his own.

A burning pain paralyzed Aiden's left arm. He aimed with the right and fired three shots into the center of Bert Welling's chest. The old man was dead.

Aiden closed his eyes and touched his upper arm where blood was already seeping through his jacket sleeve. When he looked up, he saw Tabitha leaning over him with the baby in her arms.

"Sorry," he said as he pushed himself up to a sitting position. "I'm going to be okay."

"Damn right, you are." Her voice was determined. "I'm not going to let you go. Not ever."

Epilogue

On Christmas morning, Tab awakened with a jolt Today would be baby Matthew's first Christmas, and she still hadn't figured out how to wrap his rocking horse. Matter of fact, she hadn't wrapped any presents. Funding for the new women's clinic had been guaranteed, and Tab had been busy— crazy busy. She never could have handled all the paperwork if it hadn't been for Misty pitching in to help.

Rolling onto her side, she reached for Aiden and felt nothing but empty space in the king-size bed that had once been *his* and now was *theirs*. He was already up? She could hardly believe it.

Though nobody would ever call him a slouch, he'd been taking advantage of his broken upper arm to slow down. And she thoroughly approved. Super-responsible Aiden deserved a break after ending the serial killer threat, not to mention losing his beloved Bell Long Ranger helicopter.

She hadn't planned to move in with him, and he hadn't actually invited her. While nursing him back to health from the broken arm and a second bullet that grazed his rib cage, she'd found herself spending a lot of time at his cabin. Without thinking about it, her clothing had taken up residence in his closet. Her music was on his sound system. Her food occupied most of the space in his refrigerator. And here she was, living in his house.

The only thing lacking was a commitment.

Even her grandma was staying at the Gabriel ranch for a few months to help out with the baby. Her property was being taken care of by good old Wally the Buffalo Man, even though Shua was here at the ranch.

Fully dressed in jeans and a black sweater, Aiden came into the bedroom and leaned over her for a long, lingering kiss. "Merry Christmas, Tabitha."

"Same to you."

Though he was no longer wearing a cast, just a brace, the use of his left arm was somewhat restricted. Lucky for her, his injuries hadn't slowed him down in the bedroom. Making love every night was more wonderful than she imagined. She'd taken advantage of his limited mobility to insist she should be on top.

"There are a bunch of presents in the closet downstairs," he said. "I think they need wrapping."

"I'd better get busy." The only gift she didn't need to wrap was the check for two thousand dollars that she and Aiden were contributing to Clinton's college fund. Misty still hadn't agreed to marry him, but he was planning their life together. After missing the birth of his son while he was hiding out near Maria Spotted Bear's cabin hoping to catch Tab when she returned for her horse, Clinton had vowed never to be apart from Misty or his child again. Next year, they would both be in college in Missoula. He would major in veterinary science, and she'd be pre-law.

"I suppose I can help," he said.

"I suppose you will." She tucked her hair behind her ears and gave him a smile. "Do you want your present right now?"

With his right hand, he unfastened the top button on her red satin pajamas—sleepwear that was sexier than anything she'd ever owned before. "I'd like to unwrap you."

"I'm not the gift."

She bounced from the bed and went to the bedroom closet. Tucked into a back corner was a square box. With great care, she'd wrapped it in silver paper with white stars and a delicate silver bow.

In five seconds flat, he demolished her pretty wrapping and tore open the box, revealing a perfect model of his old helicopter. "It's great," he said.

"You taught me how to fly." She kissed him on the forehead. "And how to touch the stars."

"Now it's time for your present." He took her hand and escorted her from the bedroom. "There's tradition taking root in this family, and I'd like to break the mold."

She had no idea what he was talking about. "Okay."

"First, there was my mom and Blake. Now, it's Misty and Clinton." He went down the staircase before her. "It seems like we're turning into a family of people who are scared to get married."

He seated her in a chair at the dining room table. She noticed his effort to create a mood with a fragrant bouquet of roses and soft music from a classical guitar. Outside the windows, she saw a fresh layer of snow on the ground. It was a white Christmas.

Aiden went down on one knee before her. "I'm not afraid of commitment, Tabitha. I want to spend my life with you. Marry me."

He opened a small black velvet box. A diamond engagement ring winked up at her.

When she looked into his dreamy gray eyes, she

didn't see a bit of hesitation or tension. He was sur
of himself. And he should be. He was the only ma
she had ever loved.

"Yes, Aiden."

They would be together. Forever.

* * * * *

Don't miss USA TODAY *bestselling author*
Cassie Miles's next gripping romantic suspense
when HOSTAGE MIDWIFE
goes on sale in February 2013.
Look for it wherever
Harlequin Intrigue books are sold!

LARGER-PRINT BOOKS!
GET 2 FREE LARGER-PRINT NOVELS PLUS
2 FREE GIFTS!

& Harlequin®

INTRIGUE®

BREATHTAKING ROMANTIC SUSPENSE

YES! Please send me 2 FREE LARGER-PRINT Harlequin Intrigue® novels and my 2 FREE gifts (gifts are worth about $10). After receiving them, if I don't wish to receive any more books, I can return the shipping statement marked "cancel." If I don't cancel, I will receive 6 brand-new novels every month and be billed just $5.24 per book in the U.S. or $5.99 per book in Canada. That's a saving of at least 13% off the cover price! It's quite a bargain! Shipping and handling is just 50¢ per book in the U.S. and 75¢ per book in Canada.* I understand that accepting the 2 free books and gifts places me under no obligation to buy anything. I can always return a shipment and cancel at any time. Even if I never buy another book, the two free books and gifts are mine to keep forever.

199/399 HDN FERE

Name	(PLEASE PRINT)	
Address		Apt. #
City	State/Prov.	Zip/Postal Code

Signature (if under 18, a parent or guardian must sign)

Mail to the **Reader Service:**
IN U.S.A.: P.O. Box 1867, Buffalo, NY 14240-1867
IN CANADA: P.O. Box 609, Fort Erie, Ontario L2A 5X3
Not valid for current subscribers to Harlequin Intrigue Larger-Print books.

Are you a subscriber to Harlequin Intrigue books
and want to receive the larger-print edition?
Call 1-800-873-8635 today or visit www.ReaderService.com.

* Terms and prices subject to change without notice. Prices do not include applicable taxes. Sales tax applicable in N.Y. Canadian residents will be charged applicable taxes. Offer not valid in Quebec. This offer is limited to one order per household. All orders subject to credit approval. Credit or debit balances in a customer's account(s) may be offset by any other outstanding balance owed by or to the customer. Please allow 4 to 6 weeks for delivery. Offer available while quantities last.

Your Privacy—The Reader Service is committed to protecting your privacy. Our Privacy Policy is available online at www.ReaderService.com or upon request from the Reader Service.

We make a portion of our mailing list available to reputable third parties that offer products we believe may interest you. If you prefer that we not exchange your name with third parties, or if you wish to clarify or modify your communication preferences, please visit us at www.ReaderService.com/consumerschoice or write to us at Reader Service Preference Service, P.O. Box 9062, Buffalo, NY 14269. Include your complete name and address.

HILP11B

FAMOUS FAMILIES

YES! Please send me the *Famous Families* collection featuring the Fortunes, the Bravos, the McCabes and the Cavanaughs. This collection will begin with 3 FREE BOOKS and 2 FREE GIFTS in my very first shipment—and more valuable free gifts will follow! My books will arrive in 8 monthly shipments until I have the entire 51-book *Famous Families* collection. I will receive 2-3 free books in each shipment and I will pay just $4.49 U.S./$5.39 CDN for each of the other 4 books in each shipment, plus $2.99 for shipping and handling.* If I decide to keep the entire collection, I'll only have paid for 32 books because 19 books are free. I understand that accepting the 3 free books and gifts places me under no obligation to buy anything. I can always return a shipment and cancel at any time. My free books and gifts are mine to keep no matter what I decide.

268 HCN 0387   468 HCN 0387

Name _____ (PLEASE PRINT) _____

Address _____ Apt. # _____

City _____ State/Prov. _____ Zip/Postal Code

Signature (if under 18, a parent or guardian must sign)

Mail to the **Reader Service:**

IN U.S.A.: P.O. Box 1867, Buffalo, NY 14240-1867
IN CANADA: P.O. Box 609, Fort Erie, Ontario L2A 5X3

* Terms and prices subject to change without notice. Prices do not include applicable taxes. Sales tax applicable in N.Y. Canadian residents will be charged applicable taxes. This offer is limited to one order per household. All orders subject to approval. Credit or debit balances in a customer's account(s) may be offset by any other outstanding balance owed by or to the customer. Please allow 4 to 6 weeks for delivery. Offer available while quantities last. Offer not available to Quebec residents.

Your Privacy— The Reader Service is committed to protecting your privacy. Our Privacy Policy is available online at www.ReaderService.com or upon request from the Reader Service.

We make a portion of our mailing list available to reputable third parties that offer products we believe may interest you. If you prefer that we not exchange your name with third parties, or if you wish to clarify or modify your communication preferences, please visit us at www.ReaderService.com/consumerschoice or write to us at Reader Service Preference Service, P.O. Box 9062, Buffalo, NY 14269. Include your complete name and address.

ReaderService.com

Manage your account online!

- Review your order history
- Manage your payments
- Update your address

---

*We've designed
the Reader Service website
just for you.*

Enjoy all the features!

- Reader excerpts from any series
- Respond to mailings and
  special monthly offers
- Discover new series available to you
- Browse the Bonus Bucks catalogue
- Share your feedback

Visit us at:

ReaderService.com